COASTAL
PURSUIT

OTHER TITLES BY AUTHOR

Gage Finley Adventures

Scavengers

Dark Descent

Buried Secrets

Deep Blue

Hurricane

Niki Finley Thrillers

First Shot

Second Best

Third Degree

Baseball Stories

Paint the Black

Sitting Dead Red

Chasing the Dream

Inside the Dugout: A collection of Baseball Stories

COASTAL PURSUIT

To Eric:
Ham bone.

There's always another story.
There's more than meets the eye.
- W. H. Auden

COASTAL PURSUIT

PROLOGUE

My lungs burned. And with every single footfall on the hard pavement, a jolt of pain ran through my legs. It started in my shins, then moved to my tired forty-year-old knees before progressing up to my quads.

I had to shoo that pain away, stuff it back deep inside. Because the man I was chasing was a criminal—one I'd been after my entire career.

Archibald Mathis was a habitual offender with a propensity for stealing anything he could get his hands on. But during the chase, Mathis had done something I didn't expect. Something beyond the pattern of his previous behaviors. Looking back though, he was out of options. The road ahead of him was blocked by shipping containers stacked parallel to the St. John's River and tucked within the Jacksonville Port Authority.

Personally, I was at a different kind of dead end. My stress and physical exhaustion level had peaked. But I had to persist because I knew I had him—he was done. As I sucked in wind, I could see the future, my life's work complete. I'd have a plaque sitting on my desk from the head of the FBI and a personal letter from the president congratulating me on the fine work of capturing one the FBI's ten most wanted.

But it was too early to be patting myself on the back. I needed to get the job done. It was my ego that got me in that position in the first place, and my ego that kept me from capturing him the last time we got close.

While I had been chasing Mathis for the better part of my FBI career, I thought about what I might say when the time came to slap the cuffs on his wrists. *Nice try, Mathis, but you're going down.*

Original, I know.

But I never even got to open my mouth to utter that sentence. The last thing I saw before the lights went out was the muzzle fire from the end of his Glock 21. Two rounds of .45 Auto struck me center mass. As I fell backward to the waiting pavement below, all I could think about was the awards and letters I would've received for his capture performing a disappearing act—like they were circling the edge of a drain and about to fall into oblivion. They were intangible, maybe lost forever. Especially if Mathis disappeared again.

He could've easily gone on to a Caribbean island somewhere or chosen to live out the rest of his life on a boat in Casablanca, Morocco.

No. That was just my dream.

And I had plenty of time for that. Especially since my consciousness was fading and Mathis was long gone.

1

HOLY HELL! I WOKE UP WITH A START, FEELING FOR MY CHEST and sucking in wind. I found it hard to fill my lungs because there was so much pain. There was dissonance between my mind and my body. How could I still be alive? Then I thought. *The vest. The Kevlar saved my life.* I was lucky I put it on. If I hadn't, I would've woken up on the other side of eternity.

I was in a hospital room. It was stark white—a white no one liked to see or would dare paint the walls of their own home for the simple fact that it looked like a hospital room.

Three windows showed me the adjoining hallway. People shuffled around, running from one job to another to keep up with the beehive of the hospital system.

To my left were more windows. Which showed me outside. What I wouldn't have given for an ocean view. I leaned forward to see, but no . . . they wouldn't do that . . . not for an underclass citizen like me—a measly FBI agent who failed to capture his man. No. My window faced the brick façade of the attached wing of the hospital.

I fell back against the bed, not hard, but hard enough to convulse at the pain in my aching chest. My breathing was labored. And as I sucked in wind, a visitor walked in.

"Well, lookey what we have here. Someone's awake."

It was Billy Lyons—a friend and fellow agent. We came up together through the ranks. Both of us were hotshot detectives in different cities when the bureau came calling and we opted for greener pastures. Well . . . maybe not greener, but more respectable—at least in our eyes.

I'd worked dozens of cases in my short time as a detective only to lose out when major crimes stepped in or the bureau took over because the crime crossed state lines. That chapped my hide, so I figured, why not join 'em?

Billy was carrying two coffees—one in each hand. I believed one was for me.

"You read my mind." I reached for the cup.

"What? This?" Billy tipped the plastic cup toward me. "I don't think so, stud. I've been double fisting this crap all day. I have to, to keep awake after your incessant moaning all night."

"I don't moan in my sleep," I said.

"The hell you say. Like a little girl." He mocked me. But I was used to it. That was how our relationship worked. I mocked him, he mocked me. It was perfect.

"Plus, the doctor says no coffee. She doesn't want anything raising your heartrate. Not after the near miss."

"She?"

He nodded and winked. "Yeah, she. She's hot too."

I rolled my eyes. Billy always did have an eye for the women. He was at ease around them. Even now when his gut was pushing beyond his belt line, the man still had game.

"Easy, tiger. I don't want you get thrown out of here for harassing my doctor."

"Relax, I'm just saying." Billy moved to the window and kept his back to me. "I take notice of the things you seem to miss."

Of course—another shot. But not about the doctor.

"What's that supposed to mean?"

He swung back around and caught my wide eyes. "What do you think it means? It means you should've waited for me. For backup. But no. Jasper James decided to go rogue. It's just like you. You always loved those cowboy movies. So cavalier, aren't you? You decided to get yourself shot square in the chest. You're lucky you had your vest on." He moved away again, this time toward the end of the bed, and muttered, "Or maybe unlucky for me."

"What's that supposed to mean?" I said.

"Nothing." He grinned, then put his index finger to his mouth to shush me and whispered. "Here comes the doctor." He winked and his eyebrows went up.

She entered the room toting her clipboard, so at first, I couldn't see her face. Her hair was pulled back into a ponytail—a silky brown. She was wearing glasses too, but only to read. She lifted them after she raised her head to talk to me.

"Mr . . ." she paused and saw Billy out of the corner of her eye. She smiled subtly, then moved to my bedside. "James," she finished her thought. "I'm Doctor Elizabeth Blakely."

I found her name tag but didn't linger there in case she thought I was noticing her figure. When we caught eyes again, I couldn't help but get lost in their color. It wasn't one I'd seen many times. They were green with hints of brown flecks. Almost the color of an emerald.

5

"You have several contusions on your ribs," she continued, "as I'm sure you've deduced from your current situation here. But let me tell you how lucky you were to survive at all. Had you not been wearing your protective vest the bullets would've pierced your chest cavity here." She pointed at the chest wrap. "And would've likely exited almost directly out your back on the same plain. Again, had you not had your vest on, the bullets would've lacerated your heart."

"Well, it's a good thing I was wearing it then, huh."

"Um, yes." She stalled. "Of course."

"Because, if I wouldn't have, I might not have been able to meet you." I smiled.

I didn't mean for it to be a come on, but . . . I wasn't at ease around women.

She rolled her eyes. Billy gave me a thumbs up and grinned from the opposite end of my bed. Of course, both were sarcastic.

"Any . . . way," Doctor Blakely continued, "I just wanted to let you know that we will be monitoring your condition over the next day or so. If there is anything you need, please don't hesitate to ask." She smiled one last time, then left.

Billy moved to the opposite side of the bed so we both could watch the doctor leave the room.

"Smooth, James," Billy said. "Real smooth."

"I wanted to say something else, but all I kept thinking about were doctor jokes. Do you think I should've led with one of those?"

"No. I don't think jokes would've been any more helpful. I think you just plain suck when it comes to talking to woman."

"Thanks for the vote of confidence."

6

"Hey." He tapped me on the shoulder. "That's what friends are for."

We shared a laugh, but then I saw Billy's eyebrows raise and the color leave his face. "Uh, oh."

"Uh, oh? What uh, oh?" I followed his gaze.

"It's Cohen," Billy said.

Deputy Director Ryann Cohen oversaw the heist unit both Billy and I were a part of. But it wasn't Billy she was coming for. No, I was the one laid up in hospital room after getting shot by the chief suspect in over a dozen thefts across the country. I gulped—I knew what was coming. I was about to take a beating from my superior officer for being a complete moron.

"Cohen." Billy nodded as she entered.

"Shut your trap, Lyons."

She was pissed. That much was easy to see by the dark demeanor she walked in with. "The hospital was supposed to call me when you woke up."

"Well . . . I—"

She wouldn't even let me finish. "You embarrassed me and the bureau. So I don't give a damn about the next words that come out of your mouth. And let me tell you something, James: if you ever, *ever*, pull another stunt like you did today, I won't just take your badge, I'll . . . I'll . . ."

Something stewed in her mind. Perhaps she was hoping to come up with something scarier. Truth was, I loved my badge. I loved doing what I did, and the only other thing scarier than losing my badge was losing my life.

"I'll kill you myself."

Oh. Maybe the badge wasn't such a loss after all. At least considering her proffered alternative.

"You don't really mean that." I didn't know why I came

with that line, but for some reason it burst out of me like a fire hose. Like I needed her reassurance.

Shock washed over her face. Then Billy added fuel to the fire. "No, she can't, she'd miss you too much."

She shook her head in disgust. "You two are unbelievable." Then she threw up her hands and turned to leave, but before she exited fully, she turned around and grinned. "For what it's worth, James, I'm glad I didn't have to bury you today."

"Me too, Cohen."

"Good. Now get some rest, because you'll be back to work on Monday."

I looked to Billy, confused. "Isn't that in like three days?"

Billy nodded.

"Yeah. We'll start you in with the bureau's therapist," she said. "Get you on track to get back into the field. That a problem?"

Therapist? I would have rather stayed in the hospital to rot then talk to someone about my feelings. About how I wanted to return the favor to Mathis. See how he liked to take two in the chest. I paused while looking at her. Maybe she was right though. Seeing someone might be best.

"Um, no. No problem," I lied.

"Good, because we've got a lead on Mathis' location."

I sat bolt upright in my bed. "Say what now?"

"Yeah. Lyons, wanna follow it up with me?"

He didn't even hesitate before he hopped up and joined Cohen at the door.

Bastard.

"Trader," I yelled.

"Hey, what can I say, you put yourself in here. Now you

have to suffer the consequences." Billy grinned, and both disappeared to run down the suspect I had spent years tracking.

2

A WOMAN SAT BEHIND A BABY GRAND PIANO AND PLAYED THE smooth sound of jazz. She was on stage and under a spotlight. There weren't many in attendance that night, but one man had a very specific appreciation for the talented musician they called Cleo.

The lounge aptly called *Club Indigo* due to the blueish hues prevalent in the establishment's themes and decoration—was an intimate locale in New Orleans, Louisiana.

Archibald Mathis could've listened to that melody until the sun rose the following morning. He closed his eyes and got lost in the song. He swayed with the music while he gripped his lowball glass of Irish whiskey.

He hadn't seen Cleo in years. They'd shared a torrid affair in Belize once. It seemed like a lifetime ago though. Four days and three nights of romantic bliss shared between two consenting adults.

He'd been younger then—impetuous and arrogant. She was young too, but just as striking and innocent as she was now. At the time of the affair, they hadn't known each other well. All he told her was he worked in shipping containers. She never asked what that meant. She just appreciated his company as much as he appreciated hers.

On that day, Mathis only thought to track her down because he needed help. During their short time together, Cleo told him her brother had somehow gotten messed up with the law. She said he was always on the wrong side of trouble. And while he sat there listening to the music, Mathis wondered if Cleo's brother had some connections in the area. Maybe had a way to get him some quick cash, or a phony passport.

After shooting a federal agent in the chest and likely killing him, Mathis knew the heat wouldn't go away. The FBI wouldn't stop until he was either caught or dead. But long before he shot Agent James, he'd made a promise to himself: he wasn't going back to prison. Not again. Not ever.

Like every other sob story you'd hear, Mathis thought he would turn clean after his release from prison—change his ways. But after falling into the same traps set up his entire life, Mathis had started hanging with old friends who quickly brought him back down the rabbit hole once again. He knew—better than anyone—old habits die hard.

When Cleo stopped playing, Mathis put his hands together and clapped louder than any other in the entire place.

"Thank you," Cleo spoke softly into the microphone. "This next song goes out to someone special to me. I didn't know him long, but . . . well . . . let's just say he left an impression. It's called 'Belize.' I hope you enjoy it."

Mathis' breath was sucked from his lungs, and he couldn't find air again. Her words filled him with admiration. Even more so than when he first walked in and saw her sitting there. He leaned forward in his seat and watched her every move.

From the first note she struck on the piano, he was entranced and transported back to their time together. Walking hand in hand on the beach. Diving Lighthouse Reef. Enjoying the local cuisine.

Then when she began to sing, he was transported back into their villa and he felt once again the passion they shared for each other.

Her voice was so smooth—so sultry.

When she finished, he stood from his chair to clap, but found himself so lightheaded that he had to return to his seat to gather himself—then try again.

"Y'all are too kind. Thank you for coming out tonight. I'm gonna to take a break for a few, but I'll be back in twenty or thirty minutes." She waved to the crowd, then the spotlight went out and she pushed herself up from the piano and walked away.

That was Mathis' chance. He had to cut her off before she made it to the break room. She walked away from him and to the back of the establishment.

"Excuse me." Mathis bumped into a chair, then a table.

The people he bumped were annoyed, but he didn't give them a second glance. He was too focused on where Cleo ended up.

When he lost sight of her, he started into a jog. Once he got around the stage, he watched her turn the corner.

"Cl—" he started to yell but realized she wouldn't hear him.

Mathis reached a corner and peeked around it to see her entering a room. A large man who had to be a bouncer—or her bodyguard—shut her inside.

Mathis didn't acknowledge the oversized beast that stood in front of the door: he was still encapsulated by Cleo's words of the song. He walked to the door and simply reached for the handle, but the man grabbed his wrist and squeezed. "Don't think so. Only talent back there."

The man's grip was tight. Mathis looked him up and down. He'd seen many men this big in prison and knew the bigger they were the harder they'd fall. He'd start by kicking out his knee. Once the beast buckled, Mathis would've given him a swift jab to the neck. Maybe he'd crush his larynx, maybe not. Either way, the Hulk would have been incapacitated.

But Mathis couldn't draw attention like that. He couldn't have the police called. No one could know his whereabouts, because the FBI would soon enough.

"Please, sir. I need to speak with her, I need to speak with Cleo."

He shook his head no.

Mathis breathed deep. "Can you give her a message?"

The man gritted his teeth. "What message?"

"Tell her Belize is outside waiting for her."

"The hell does that mean?"

"Just tell her." Mathis grinned.

The man eyed him awkwardly.

"Please. I beg you."

The bodyguard opened the door and stepped inside.

Mathis primped himself, making sure his apparel was up to standard and the backpack he carried slung around his back stayed in place.

He didn't have to wait long. When the door opened, Mathis expected to see the big man return, but instead it was Cleo. She looked into his eyes and grinned wide. Then she threw her arms around his neck.

He loved the feel of her touch pushing against him. His heart pounded through his shirt.

"What are you doing here?" She pushed out of the hug.

Mathis watched as the bodyguard returned and eyed him skeptically.

"Is there a place when can go and talk?" Mathis said.

She looked around, then suggested he follow. She grabbed him by the hand and led him through the door where the bodyguard stopped him—into the innards of the lounge. Kegs where strewn about in the hallway, and old black and white photos of famous jazz musicians were hung on the wall.

At the end of the hall was another door. With each passing step, excitement grew in his belly. Maybe it was from the touch of her hand. He hadn't felt hers in some time.

When they reached her room, she pushed inward and walked inside. Immediately she spun around and faced him. She stood close—close enough for him to feel her breath on his lips. He lingered there, unwilling to say something in fear he'd ruin the moment.

But she didn't wait. Cleo pressed her lips against his, and it felt so right. His belly spun—in a good way. That was exactly what he wanted, but it wasn't what he needed in that moment. He was crunched for time. But he didn't want to stop.

And it seemed, neither did she.

3

As they lay on the couch inside the room close together, Cleo looked deep into Mathis' eyes. "How did you find me?"

"The sign outside said, '*Tonight Only Featuring: Cleo.*'"

She chuckled. "Okay, wise guy. I mean, how did you know I'd be here tonight?"

Mathis shrugged. "Luck, I suppose."

Then she turned and rested her head on his bare chest. She must have been able to hear his heart pounding.

Mathis stroked her long dark hair, remembering how she fancied it. It calmed her—made her feel loved. He wanted to ask about her brother but couldn't then.

After two minutes of silence, Cleo found his eyes again. "How long are you in town for?"

As he stared at the caramel coloring of her irises, he knew she had him wrapped around her finger. He knew he couldn't lie to her. "Not long."

Her face fell and she pushed onto her elbows and off his

chest, then placed her bare feet on the floor. She waited to speak. Maybe to gather the right words.

"Then why come all the way here? To tease me and leave me?"

"No." Mathis reached for her, but she rose from the couch and walked to the opposite side of the room to grab a kimono robe.

"Wait." Mathis rose too.

She whipped around and said, "For what?"

"I'm sorry, I didn't mean to . . ." he trailed off.

"To what?"

Mathis swallowed hard and dropped his head. He never intended to hurt her. If he could only explain his situation. Tell her what was happening. But how could he? She didn't know he was a thief and now a potential murderer.

"Talk." Her tone shifted from annoyed to angry. "And you better hurry, because I only have a few minutes before I need to be back on stage."

Mathis knew the conversation would take longer than just a couple minutes. "Can we talk after your show?"

Her hands were on her hips, and she tilted her head to the side. "Fine. I'll meet you at the bar. And your explanation better be worth the wait."

Mathis caught his breath. "Thank you. And it will be."

"Now, if you don't mind, I need to get ready, so . . ." Cleo nodded to the door.

"I'll show myself out." Mathis lifted his clothes and pack, then made his exit.

As the door shut, he glanced back one more time, hoping he hadn't screwed up his shot with the only woman he ever loved.

. . .

THE REMAINING songs on Cleo's setlist changed their tune. Only songs of pain, sadness, and anger danced across the ivory keys. Still though, Mathis appreciated the music—more importantly, the musician.

During the final song, Mathis thought, *what if*? Maybe she would come along if he asked. Go somewhere out of the country. But that would mean he would need to tell her the whole truth. Tell her what happened after their affair in Belize all those years ago. Why he disappeared. And how much trouble he was really in.

He was lost in his thoughts when the last note on the piano fell. Amongst the clapping, Mathis shook from his trance and watched her dismount the stage and walk toward his seat at the bar.

As she walked, people begin to file out of the lounge. It was near closing time. Had to be. Mathis glanced at his watch.

1:30 a.m.

He didn't see the bartender set a glass down on the bar. Cleo walked right toward him and picked up the full glass of water. She downed it in one gulp before she even spoke a word to him.

"So . . . out with it." She looked at him with contempt.

Mathis leaned in close. In a soft whisper and amongst the ambient noise of the patrons and their bar talk, he said, "I'm a thief."

She scrunched her brow in disbelief. Mathis wondered if she heard him because she remained quiet. But he wasn't about to say it again, not in a public bar.

"A thief?" She gave him a sideways glance.

He nodded.

Another glass of water was set in front of her. She took it

in her hand, then stared at her own reflection in the mirror behind the bar.

"What are you thinking?" Mathis had to know.

She was lost in thought. The anticipation was killing him. But it didn't seem that she cared. Her response would be on her own time.

Then she showed him her back and walked away.

Mathis jumped from the stool and followed her. She sidestepped the final group of people who had congregated in the middle of the bar. Mathis kept pace. He wanted to reach out and stop her, but he couldn't. Again, he didn't want to cause a scene if she reacted poorly to his touch.

When she exited the lounge, she pushed through the door and walked into the night.

Her pace quickened once outside. Mathis chased her down Bourbon Street for the better part of a block before she spun around and slapped him across the face.

"A thief? You bastard. How dare you?" She hit him again, this time in the chest. "I cared for you. Wrote a song about us—about Belize. How could I fall for a thief?"

A tear fell from her eye. Her fists pounded him again. Mathis took the shots until she was so wrapped up in emotion that she fell into his arms. He pulled her close as she continued to weep.

Again, Mathis didn't speak. He was afraid to. Afraid to say something else that would make her run.

She pulled away from his chest and said, "You're in trouble, aren't you?"

Mathis nodded.

"How much?"

"The deepest."

"That's why you came to me, isn't it?" It was so easy for

her to read him. Even after all their time apart. "I know I'm gonna regret this, but . . . how can I help?"

Shocked, Mathis stepped back to catch his breath. He didn't want to ask this favor. Deep down, he didn't really want to involve her at all, but under the circumstances, what choice did he have?

"Does your brother live close?"

"My brother?" She crinkled her brow.

Mathis nodded.

"What do you want with him?"

"Well, it's just . . . you said . . . when we were in Belize . . . that he's on the wrong side of the law . . . and I just figured —" Mathis cut himself off.

She filled in the rest. "He was. He's doing ten years for B & E. Sounds like y'all would have a lot in common."

Her dig cut him. But it was spot on and he deserved it.

Mathis's head fell.

She clenched her jaw and waited. Holding something back. She let out an exasperated huff, then said, "But I might have another friend who could help you."

"Really? Who?" Mathis didn't mean to sound excited, but he did.

"Her name is Veronica."

"Her name?"

"That's right. Is that a problem?"

"No. Not, at all. Can we see her tonight?"

"She won't be back into town for three days."

"Three days?" Mathis couldn't mask his disappointment.

"Yeah, she's in Jamaica on her honeymoon."

"Her honeymoon?"

Cleo nodded. "Yes. And she gets back in three days."

Mathis held his breath. Then pushed it out and said, "I don't know if I can wait that long."

Sharp as a whip, Cleo said, "That's not my problem. Or hers. You got yourself into this mess. And she's all I have. Take it or leave it."

"I'll take it." Mathis stared at her, ensnared by her beauty as they locked eyes. He was hopeful he could stay with her. "You don't happen to have a place to stay, do you?"

"Nope. You're on your own. Meet me back here. Same time, same place three days from now. I'll have Veronica with me. Don't be late or we'll be gone."

"Thank you," Mathis said.

But Cleo didn't say, "you're welcome." She simply turned and walked into the darkness of Bourbon Street until she reached a corner and disappeared into the night.

4

The sound of a pen scribbling over paper set my hair on end. I hated being there. Hated sitting in the comfortable chair while Dr. Morgan judged me. He'd only asked one question. Then he went into a writing tizzy for the better part of three minutes.

What could he have possibly been writing? I mean, the man asked me what I had for breakfast. Of course, I answered with my usual: nothing except coffee. Black with a splash of sweet cream.

That had been my breakfast for almost fifteen years. Ever since my first cup when I joined the police force back in Minneapolis when I was a rookie.

How could my answer possibly have sent him into a mile-long monologue inside his own head?

"So . . ." He still ogled his notebook before he finished. Then he looked up to me again. "Do you have any negative thoughts?"

Negative thoughts? What the hell did that mean? I was having some pretty negative thoughts then, but they weren't brought on by the stress of getting shot in the chest. They were boiling over due to the fact the FBI was forcing me to sit there and listen to that nonsense.

"Negative thoughts?" I questioned.

Maybe I'd get somewhere if I answered his question with one of my own.

"Any thoughts of suicide? Anything like that?"

If I was to be honest . . . maybe in the past I'd thought like that, but not then. I got right with the Lord from the PTSD I endured in my younger life—shame from abuse when I was a child. That was what spurred the devil on. Since then though, I hadn't had a single thought of taking my own life.

"No. Nothing like that."

Dr. Morgan went back to his notes, and I took that opportunity to stare around the room. I'd only visited his office a few times. You know the drill, whenever you discharged your weapon in the line of duty, they'd always send you to meet with Dr. Morgan to make sure your mind was right before he'd stamp the approval form and allow you back into the field to chase down bad guys.

A picture of Yogi Berra hung on the wall. He was by himself smiling his usual wide and happy grin. I looked closer. There was an inscription toward the bottom. I couldn't read it from where I sat, but I had to get up because I too was a baseball fan. I didn't much care for the Yankees, but you must respect any franchise that has as many championships as they have.

The inscription read: "To Mitchell, it ain't over till it's over."

A classic Yogism, but why did he sign it that way, I wondered? But I wanted to make sure of something first.

Sure enough, the diplomas on the wall each had the name Mitchell Morgan. One from Stanford—another from Yale. I curled my lower lip. *The doc's got more credibility than I thought.*

"Did you know Yogi Berra?" I spun around to ask, but hadn't realized he'd risen from his chair and joined me by the picture.

"Knew him." He chuckled. "That's a loose term. Let's just say my father and he were acquaintances."

"Oh, I see. What's with the inscription?"

Dr. Morgan stared at the picture. As I studied his reaction, his face went blank. Like he was lost in thoughts of time passed.

What he said next I never expected.

"When I was young, I was diagnosed with cancer— Hodgkin's Lymphoma."

A wave of shock passed over me. "I'm sorry."

"Oh, don't be." He downplayed my apology with a wave of his hand. "I'm fine now. But back then, my father reached out to Mr. Berra. He ended up signing this picture for me." He nodded toward it. "Naturally, being a Yankees fan, I've carried it with me wherever I've gone." He paused, then turned back into the center of the room and said, "But enough about me. Shall we?"

After I returned to my seat, I let down my guard. I figured, why not? We'd bonded over the picture and his willingness to demonstrate vulnerability. He wasn't some stiff in a cardigan out to keep me from my life's purpose of tracking down Mathis once and for all.

"So . . . tell me about Agent Lyons." Dr. Morgan said.

"Billy?"

Dr. Morgan nodded at my dimwittedness. As if he didn't

know.

"Well, he's . . ." I trailed off. I couldn't think of anything to say that wasn't a crack at him. Only until, one word came to mind: family. "He's like a brother to me."

Dr. Morgan nodded. "And is that a good thing?"

A good thing? Why wouldn't it be. "Yeah, sure, why not?" I said.

"I just mean . . . do you feel like you're too close?"

"Too close?" I said. What was he getting at?

He continued. "Some agents feel that if you get too close to your partners, you're more afraid to bring them into dangerous situations. Like you'd be afraid to lose them."

"Afraid to lose him?" I asked. I'd never felt like that. *At least not until now, you dick.*

"That's right."

I ruminated a moment, thinking what to say next. Why did he even ask the question to begin with? But before I spoke again, he followed up with another question.

"Is that why you went after Mathis alone. Because you didn't want to put Agent Lyons in danger."

"What? No. Of course not. That's ridiculous," I said, but then thought, *wait . . . was it?* I didn't really have a reason not to wait for Billy. Not to wait for backup. Maybe if I did, I wouldn't have gotten shot.

Then the devil twisted my mind. *Or maybe Billy would've.*

I needed to answer again. Set the record straight. "No. I went after him because I had a trail on him. I knew if I waited, he would vanish again. Like he did before when we got close. I knew I could get to him this time. Track him down and slap the cuffs on. When I got close, he stopped and then . . ." A lump grew in my throat and my words got stuck there.

"But then he shot you instead," Dr. Morgan filled in the blanks.

"Yeah." I nodded, but then bowed in humiliation. I didn't know why, but I did feel humiliated. Ashamed of being outwitted by a foe. As an FBI agent, I was supposed to have the upper hand in every situation. That was what I was trained for. But with the case of Mathis, I didn't.

"Tell me about your ex-wife."

There it was. A gut punch. One I didn't figure I'd hear during that conversation. "What does she have to do with this?"

But Dr. Morgan didn't answer. He just sat and looked at me. Maybe he expected me to lead the conversation. Like an idiot, I obliged.

"She left me four years ago."

"Why?"

Because I was an asshole. But I couldn't say that. I couldn't admit it to anyone else. Not then, anyway.

"I think she thought it seemed like a good idea."

"Sounds rash. Was there any reason other than that?" he said.

Multiple. Probably started with me being closed off and unwilling to share my feelings with her. I'd get sucked into my work. I put her on the back burner and wouldn't let her in on my secrets. But the only thing I told the doctor was, "Sometimes people just aren't meant to be."

Truth was, I would've taken Claire back in an instant if she would've had me, but that ship had sailed, as they say. She remarried and had a child. She was happier without me.

Dr. Morgan nodded and bit his lower lip. He could see

right through me. I mean, I didn't even believe the crap I was spouting off. Even after we had bonded over baseball.

"I'm going to need to see you again before I can approve you to return to the field."

"Seriously? Why?"

"Because you haven't been forthright with me."

"What else is there to say?" There was plenty.

"Let's just save that for next time, shall we?"

"Next time? But what about Mathis? I need to catch him before he leaves the country."

"How do you know he'll leave the country?"

"That's what he does after a heist. And even now . . . after he shot me." I rubbed my chest.

"How do you know he hasn't left already?"

He was right. How could I know? So far, Billy and Cohen hadn't come up with anything. They'd followed the lead after they left me in the hospital room, but it led nowhere.

"I don't."

"There you have it. You don't. So . . . like I said, I'll need to see you again."

I jumped from my seat then said, "How's tomorrow?"

"I'll check my schedule and get back to you."

I walked toward the door, and when I reached it, Dr. Morgan said, "No matter when we meet again, Agent James, I'd appreciate it if you'd come with an open mind and willingness to share."

I wondered why he told me that.

"Because if you can, it will expedite this process." He winked, then fell back into his office and finally took a seat at his desk.

I guess I found my answer.

5

MATHIS STARED AT HIMSELF IN THE MIRROR, MAKING SURE HIS appearance was appropriate for his meeting with Cleo and the mysterious Veronica. He pulled the black ball cap down tight over his head. He hadn't worn many hats in his lifetime—he did then only to mask his identity.

After trying on a pair of sunglasses, he immediately took them off. He couldn't wear those, not in the middle of the night. Even though Corey Hart might have thought it was cool, Mathis would draw unnecessary attention. The hat was enough.

He'd only left his dirty motel room once since the night he met Cleo. And after three days of being cooped up and eating nothing but bad takeout, Mathis was thrilled to leave the filth behind.

The air was thick and humid, even at the late hour of the night. Mathis searched the ground below as he walked across the second story walkway of the motel. There were people outside being loud and obnoxious. Probably the same people he'd heard each night since his arrival.

There were two women and one man. The women were dressed in short skirts, and the man was draped in attire that would've made Shaft jealous.

Mathis avoided eye contact, but that didn't stop one of the women from calling out to him. "Hey, sweetie."

The click of her high heels echoed off the asphalt. Mathis didn't stop, or turn to acknowledge her, even though she'd clearly spoken only to him.

He kept walking, getting close to the sidewalk and within about thirty feet from where the two women and the man stood.

"Hey, hon, I'ma talkin' ta you," she sounded irritated.

Then it was the man who spoke. His tone fell harsher. "Yo bro, slow ya roll. What's the matter, you don't like women?"

Mathis picked up speed and accelerated into a run.

"Look at him go. He running away," the man laughed. They all laughed.

Mathis hated fleeing like a coward. He had no problem defending himself, but again, he couldn't have a dispute. He *couldn't* be late. Nothing was going to stop him from meeting Cleo.

HUNDREDS OF PEOPLE swarmed the streets of New Orleans at the late hour. Mathis wondered how he would see Cleo and Veronica amongst the crowd. He looked up to the street sign again—for the third time—the intersection of Bourbon Street and St. Peter.

Glancing at his watch, he shook his head in disbelief and muttered to himself, "What the hell? Where are they?"

Rising on his tip toes, Mathis noticed two women

walking toward him. He couldn't tell if it was Cleo from where he stood.

"Excuse me." He pushed around a man and started walking to meet the ladies but stalled. He knew he couldn't leave the corner. Cleo had specifically told him same time, same place.

If he was one minute late, she would leave.

Lucky for him, he stayed put. Because as he searched— still looking for the two women who walked together— there was a soft touch on his back.

Mathis whipped around to see Cleo. Immediately he smiled. She returned with a forced smile of her own.

"Archie this is Veronica." Cleo motioned to the woman by her side.

Mathis' mouth gaped. But only for a moment when he realized he was being rude. "Archibald Mathis." He reached out his hand.

She waited for a moment, which gave Mathis time to look her over. The woman was big. Not heavyset, but near six feet tall and very muscular. She looked like a body-builder.

Veronica grabbed his hand, but instead of shaking it, she pulled hard and drew him in close to her mouth so she could whisper in his ear. "If I even suspect for one minute that you won't be truthful with me or Cleo . . . I'll cut your damn balls off with a rusty butter knife."

Stunned, Mathis peeled away. He didn't know how to react to Veronica's warning, or how much truth either of them were looking for. So, he grinned and nodded nervously, secretly wondering if Veronica was being serious or if her threat was idle.

From the looks of her, Mathis figured her to be a woman of her word.

"Follow me," Veronica said.

Mathis thought he was being chivalrous by allowing Cleo to follow first. He tried smiling at her again, but all she did was roll her pretty eyes.

Veronica led Mathis to a light blue Cadillac sedan. Parked under a streetlight. Mathis could see there was someone inside the vehicle. He stopped walking and wouldn't approach, not until he received an explanation.

Cleo saw him pause. "What are you doing, come on."

"What's with the guy? Who's he? Police? FBI?" Mathis nodded at the shadowy figure in the front seat.

"Don't be an idiot. If I wanted to turn you in, I wouldn't have brought Veronica to Bourbon Street, I would've brought the cops. I told you, Veronica just returned from her honeymoon."

"Yeah, so?" Mathis said.

"So, Einstein . . . that's my husband." Veronica tapped on the ceiling of the car.

Mathis watched a man exit. He didn't say anything. He didn't need to. His appearance spoke for itself. The beast was over six foot five and pushing 320 pounds. Like his new bride, not fat, but extremely muscular.

Mathis gulped.

"Now. Do you want to get out of here or what?" Veronica said.

He did. But getting in a car with that specific husband and wife was more than daunting.

Mathis slid in the seat behind Veronica, and Cleo sat behind the behemoth. Before the man could shift into gear, Mathis asked, "So . . . where we headed?"

"A little place outside the city."

"How far?"

"Thirty miles," Veronica said.

"Thirty miles." Mathis' voice went up into a shout. "Why so far?"

"It's where we live. Out in the bayou. Now if you don't mind, shut your damn mouth. And *enough* with the questions."

Mathis wanted to say more, but the words got stuck in his throat. He turned and caught a glimpse of Cleo's eye. But just as he looked, she shifted her attention back out the window. He did the same before slumping hard against the seat.

THE CITY PASSED by in a blur as they traveled west, and after twenty minutes with the Big Easy far behind them, Mathis couldn't help but notice the swamps and marshes that were highlighted in the murky space behind each passing streetlight.

A thought occurred to him, and he didn't know why. Men. Women. Who knew how many people could've been dumped to die in the barren wasteland of water and muck? Mathis couldn't help but wonder if that was what this was. Was he being led to his death?

He shook that thought away as fast as it came. No way Cleo would do that to him. Not after what they'd been through . . . what they'd shared.

Could she?

6
———

THE BIG MAN DRIVING SLOWED TO A ROLL. MATHIS STARED out the window and saw one lone light shining from the entry of the home. The light was dim—a muted yellow color. In the driveway—if you could call it a driveway at all —the car rolled over bent weeds and the tire marks notched perfectly with those made from past imprints.

Once stopped, the big man and Veronica glared over their shoulders.

"We're going inside, but we won't be staying for long," Veronica said.

Mathis scrunched his brow, wondering what her intentions were.

"Now come on. I don't want you lingering about. Not with the amount of heat that's on you. Have you seen the news lately?" Veronica asked.

"I have," Mathis said.

"Your picture is plastered all over the place. I'm actually surprised you weren't recognized on Bourbon Street."

"That's why I wore the ball cap," Mathis said. "And why we met at night."

"Sure, sure. Whatever. All I know is, I don't want you hanging around me or Cleo any longer. This is a one-time deal. You get me?" Veronica said.

Mathis nodded. "I understand."

"Good," Veronica said, then she opened her door and everyone else followed suit.

The sound of croaking bullfrogs and popping cicadas echoed underneath the moonlit sky. As Mathis stepped carefully through the thick grass, he was reminded of his youth. When he was no more than ten, he'd hiked through the Louisiana bayou with a group of his friends. While near the water, he stepped close to a water moccasin. The snake struck him in the calf, and he was rushed to the hospital to receive antivenom to save his life. From that moment on, he was careful to look where he stepped.

The closer they came to the entrance, more of the house revealed itself. The siding was decaying—weathered by time and salty air. When the big man pulled on the screen door, it screeched loudly and dropped out of place as a hinge let loose.

He stuck his big butt out and held the door open for his wife as she turned the deadbolt.

Veronica entered first, followed by Cleo, then Mathis, and finally the big man. When they got inside, Mathis and Cleo didn't enter far. Only Veronica ventured deeper, hopefully looking for a light. The door clanged shut and Mathis jumped in place, startled by the crash.

A light sparked to life—one lone bulb hung down from the ceiling. Mathis stared at the bulb, then shifted his attention to the room itself. It was empty. No TV. No furniture.

Nothing. Nothing, but chipping paint and pealing flower-printed wallpaper.

Mathis shook his head up and down, judging the place. "It sure is . . . homey here."

"Blow it outcha ass, bluto. It's da safe house," the big man said.

"Safe house?" Mathis said and stared at the big man. "From what?"

"The government," Veronica supplied as she walked back into the entryway.

"The government?" Mathis was confused. "What are you—" Mathis cut himself off before he asked a question he'd regret. "Never mind."

"Smart man," Veronica said. "Now. Follow me."

Veronica led them through the kitchen. It was clean, but again, lacking essentials. The only thing there was a folding table and chairs stacked neatly in the corner. As she continued to walk, Mathis couldn't help but notice Cleo. She kept pace with Veronica and didn't once turn around to offer a smile to Mathis. Maybe she wanted nothing else to do with him, *but then*, he thought*, at least she's helping. Maybe she still does care? At least a little.*

Mathis reached for her arm, to spin her and make her stop so they could talk more. Hash out what was on her mind. But before he could touch her skin, Veronica walked through the back door and into the back yard.

Another light was on, much like the one in the front yard. A dim muted yellow. But it was bright enough to showcase two boat slips. There was a small skiff at one, and an airboat docked at the other. The house backed to a bayou or some kind of waterway.

Veronica stopped and opened her arm.

"What's this?" Mathis paused alongside her.

"Your ticket out of here."

"What? That?" Mathis chuckled and nodded to the skiff. Then he returned his attention back to Veronica.

She wasn't laughing.

Mathis marched forward to see the actual size of the boat. In the dark, it looked abnormally small.

His fears were confirmed.

The boat couldn't have been longer than twelve feet. It had an old motor—about the same age as the house, from the looks of it.

"She done me well in the past. Poaching gators," the big man said.

Mathis returned his attention back on the others. "That's great, but I'm not gonna have time for that. I need to run."

"And run you can. Thanks to them." Now it was Cleo who spoke up for her friends.

Mathis sighed.

"What am I supposed to do once I make it to the ocean?"

"Pray you don't get stuck in a hurricane." Veronica roared with laughter. The others followed suit. Everyone but Mathis was clearly entertained.

"Ha ha. Funny," Mathis muttered under his breath. He continued to look at the boat. Then he saw the airboat. That was no use, not on open water. He had no choice. They really had done him a solid. They didn't have to lend him their boat. Perhaps though, in his mind, the favor that Cleo promised was a little nicer than a twelve-foot skiff with a broken-down motor.

Mathis quickly turned his attention back on Cleo. He

walked directly toward her and stood tall. He glanced at Veronica and her husband, then said, "Can we talk alone?"

All remained silent, waiting for Cleo to answer for herself. She nodded yes. Mathis didn't hesitate. He grabbed her by the hand and led her toward the shoreline. "Come with me," he said.

She stayed silent. Which give him pause to beg.

"Please. I know you don't trust me, but we'll make it. I swear."

"How can you be sure? Ten seconds ago, you asked what to do once you got into open water."

"That was ten seconds ago."

"So now what . . . you have the confidence of a reckless teenage boy?"

"That's what you make me feel like."

She grinned, but it was masked by the night sky. "Always the man with the right words to say."

Mathis reached for her hands. He held them gently. "I need you, Cleo," Mathis said.

There was emotion behind her voice when she spoke next. "I . . . I don't think I can. We'd be fugitives together. With no money—no country to call home."

"This land has always seemed foreign to me anyhow." He was grasping at straws, but he would say anything to get her to come.

She dropped her head and said, "Sorry, I . . . I just can't."

Mathis sighed and pulled his hand free from hers.

Veronica and the big man returned to Cleo's side.

"I think it's best you leave," Veronica said.

Before he could step into the boat, Cleo backed away from Veronica's side and threw herself into Mathis's chest. Her momentum knocked him off-balance, but he caught himself before falling into the swamp. She held him tight, and he hugged her back. When she pushed out of the hug, she handed him an envelope.

"What's this?" he said.

"A parting gift."

The envelope was thick. Like a wad of money or stacked paper. He wanted to open it, but the anticipation of what lay inside gave him the motivation he needed to continue onward, at least until first light.

Once aboard, the big man shoved the bow and launched the boat into the calm bayou.

Mathis ripped the cord of the old motor, and wouldn't you know it, it started on the first pull.

"I guess luck's on my side," Mathis muttered to himself.

He steered the vessel away from the shoreline when the big guy said, "Spotlight's on the bow. You need it to see."

Mathis leaned forward and switched the light on.

"Watch out for dem gators," the big man called into the night.

"And the Coast Guard," Veronica sneered.

"Coast Guard," Mathis said to himself, knowing that was the truest of possibilities.

7

MY EYES WERE HEAVY AS I STARED AT THE BLINKING CURSOR on the computer screen of my laptop, but I had to continue until I found something. Of course, I was logged into the FBI's database with Billy's username and password. I'd known both since the beginning of our friendship. I hadn't stolen them: he had mine too for times such as those. But I mean come on, if I'd wanted to steal it, it wouldn't have been that difficult. The man still used his mother's maiden name for the password. Who does that?

As I pondered, I wondered how Mathis escaped after he shot me. We were the United States government. How could we not track him down? Cameras had him leaving Jaxport in a midsized black sedan. Sure, he probably dumped the car not far from there, but still, there were highway cameras everywhere in Jacksonville. Damn near in every direction.

Statistically, he would've gone farther south to find a way out of the country. Find some stashed boat down A1A or a harbor fleet. For some reason though, my gut told me he went north. Especially after Billy and Cohen came up emptyhanded chasing down a lead in Daytona Beach.

What scared me most was it had been days since anyone had last seen him. And as any good detective knows, if a crime isn't solved within the first forty-eight hours, it likely will remain unsolved.

I had perused everything the database had on Mathis and found nothing.

Not until I happened across a picture. The photograph was one we found in Mathis's old apartment—one we'd searched only days after he vacated the premises back in 2014.

The picture was of a lone woman. A young beautiful woman with olive skin and thick, dark brown hair she tousled her hands through. She was being playful with the camera, or maybe the person behind the lens. I knew she wasn't some random woman. Not a sister. Not a friend. This was someone Mathis cared for more than that—a lover.

I must've seen the picture a hundred times over the years, but there was one thing I'd always missed. At least until then. Through her dark hair, I could see a tattoo on her wrist. I tilted my head and squinted, but I still couldn't quite make out the word. It looked like letters. There were at least three.

Were they initials?

I zoomed in to enhance the photo, but there was only so much I could do with my ancient laptop. One the bureau provided me with, mind you.

The last letter was an A. What was strange though was all the letters were capitals. Next to the A was an L. Then only half the next letter was shown. Maybe it was a number, I couldn't tell.

Maybe A, L, O?

"OLA? What hell does that mean?"

I racked my brain for anything. But as I continued to stare at my computer screen, the white space began to morph and fade away. My eyes drooped and I yawned.

When I looked at the clock, I realized it was late. Past three a.m. "Damn," I said.

I had an appointment with the FBI psychologist again. He'd got me in early. And I had to be at his office by seven.

Sleep was best at that moment. I knew it to be true.

I shut my laptop and fell on my pillow.

As I laid there for a moment, I closed my eyes. Just as I did one word popped into my head: NOLA.

New Orleans, Louisiana.

Had to be. What else could the initials stand for?

I jumped from my prone position and reached for the phone.

The phone rang. And rang. And rang. "Come on, you bastard, pick up."

"Why are you calling me?" Not even a greeting, the old Scrooge. "Aren't you still on suspension?"

"Yeah, but I think I found something."

"Jasper, it's three o'clock in the morning."

"This couldn't wait."

"Obviously."

"I know where Mathis is."

"How? Have you been logging in under my name again?"

"Of course, but that's beside the point."

"Says the man who's been illegally hacking into the FBI."

"Illegally?" I laughed. "You're the one that gave me the login info."

"Oh, yeah," Billy said. "So . . . tell me wise guy, how do *you* know where he is?"

"He's in New Orleans."

"What? Why would he go there?"

"You remember the girl from his file?"

Without missing a beat, Billy said, "The fine brunette?"

"Yeah, her."

"Sure, what of her?"

"She lives there. Or she's at least from there."

"How do you know that? We don't even know her name, or her connection to Mathis. Maybe she was just some model he got off on."

"No. I'm telling you, they had a relationship."

"Okay . . . but that still doesn't add up. Why her? Why New Orleans?"

"The tattoo."

"The one on her wrist?"

"Yeah."

"It's just initials."

"That's what I thought too, but when I was lying in bed, it just hit me. What if there were more than three letters? What could they spell?"

"I'm pretty sure 'New Orleans' wouldn't fit on her wrist."

"No shit, Sherlock, but what about NOLA?"

"NOLA? What the hell does that mean?"

"New Orleans, Louisiana." Billy paused on the other end. Maybe for effect, or maybe he fell asleep. "Am I boring you?" I teased.

"No. Just processing."

"And?"

"I'll bring it to Cohen in the morning. See what she says."

"That's my man."

"I am your man, and don't you forget it."

"Don't tease me."

Then Billy spoke with clarity, and maybe a little pride. "You do know if this pans out, you won't be able to take any credit for it."

I thought for a moment. It was true. Obviously, I couldn't. But that didn't bother me. "Hey as long as we bury the bastard, or lock him behind bars, I'm fine with that."

"If you say so," he said.

8

THE OCEAN SLAPPED AGAINST THE HULL OF THE BOAT, SENDING particles of sea water flying through the air before splashing against Mathis' face. The combination of the sun's warmth and wetness on his skin jolted him awake as he leaned on his arm.

He hadn't meant to doze off and it might have happened more than once as he steered away from the bayous of Louisiana and into the Gulf of Mexico. He paralleled the coast of Alabama, maybe Florida, he couldn't be certain. One thing was for sure, he was farther offshore than he intended to be.

Mathis twisted the throttle of the tiller steer outboard motor, and it sputtered—like it was running low on fuel.

"Oh, don't you fail on me now." He rubbed the outer shell casing of the motor for good luck and glanced toward shore.

He was forced with a decision: beach the vessel and take his chances on land, or takes his chances drifting when the fuel ran out.

If he beached the vessel on land, maybe he could find another boat. A yacht, or sailboat. Something bigger he could steal. To cruise deep into the Gulf. Go to Mexico. Central America. Or even the Caribbean.

Drifting without a rudder would most certainly end in disaster. He'd be at the mercy of the current and wind. In addition, the Coast Guard patrolled those waters. If they happened to get lucky—especially in their heightened sense of alert due to a federal fugitive on the lam—he'd be screwed.

In hindsight, he should've asked the big man or Veronica if they had an extra tank of gasoline. Then he thought, maybe there was an extra one. When he left in the dark of night, he hadn't bothered to look. Maybe another was hiding.

Mathis fell off the bench seat and ripped open the compartment under the motor.

"Damn."

Only one.

Mathis recaptured sight of the beach. There wasn't a single soul there. Not at that hour at least. Maybe the beach was private? He could only hope.

Mathis steered toward the white sand. He was close, probably two hundred yards offshore. Nothing stood out beyond the sand—not until he rode a wave as it crashed toward shore. There was movement at a house. A person shifted from their perched position on their patio. They must've been watching the early morning surf before they were interrupted by some lowlife trying to trespass on their private property.

"Hey. What the hell do you think you're doing?" the man

screamed, but most of the noise was drowned out by the rolling waves and the rumble of the outboard.

Mathis turned the motor to the starboard side, directly into the cresting wave. The boat took on water, and Mathis took a shot of salty sea to the face.

He was lucky to keep the boat afloat as he rode the crest before turning away from the beach.

Again, the motor sputtered, then stalled. "No. No," he said aloud. "Not yet. Not now."

Mathis let off the throttle for a moment to let the motor catch its breath before the smoke choked the life out of it. Once the sputtering stopped, he gently twisted the throttle and continued. He was careful not to get too far from shore in case the motor finally gave out.

As he continued, there were no more homes that lined the shoreline, but instead a collection of high-rise buildings. No doubt condos for the snowbirds from up north. With more residences, there would be more chances of encountering people.

Mathis' sphincter puckered at the prospect of coming up on a crowded beach. Someone would recognize him.

There was a family playing in the sand. A young couple and two kids—twins, by the looks of it. They couldn't have been older than seven. Maybe eight. Mathis avoided eye contact even though he heard one of them say, "Mom look, a boat."

Mathis kept his eyes trained ahead. On the horizon there was a jutting peninsula of rock—an inlet.

Immediately, Mathis recognized the area. He was near Orange Beach. Almost to the Alabama-Florida state line. If he continued his current path, soon he'd be in Perdido Key.

That was probably the last place he wanted to beach a vessel—there was a naval base just up the road in Pensacola. Finding a way to blend in at the marina near Orange Beach was his only option. And with the mass amounts of hotels, restaurants, and private residences equipped with boat slips, that listed a host of potential hiding spots.

"This will work out just fine," Mathis said to himself as he steered around the rock and grinned. "I guess someone up there is looking out for me." He glanced toward the sky.

But just as Mathis rounded the corner, a thirty-two-foot special purpose patrol boat flipped its sirens on. The sound echoed over the water. And the vessel rushed directly toward Mathis' position in the water.

9

WALKING BACK INTO THE BUILDING THAT I LEFT ONLY DAYS prior felt somehow . . . foreign. Sure, I was walking in with bruised ribs and a thick wrap around my chest, but that wasn't the reason it felt weird. But as soon as I saw Billy sitting behind his desk, that strangeness—that feeling of being out of place—faded like a mist in a windstorm.

I walked over for a greeting. His head was down and he didn't see me standing there, but he could sense someone lingered.

"Can I help you?" he didn't bother to look up. He just went on writing in his notes.

I turned my head to see what he was writing. Honestly, I couldn't tell. My ability to read upside down had never been exceptional.

"I sure as hell hope so, Special Agent Lyons."

His pen fell to the paper. He stalled, then caught my eye and smiled.

"The doc clear you?" He knew that was the only way I'd be allowed back in the building.

"This morning."

Billy pushed out from behind his desk and walked around to meet me. He grabbed my hand and shook it then pulled me in close for one of his famous bear hugs.

When he released me from the hug, I asked, "Did you bring my theory to Cohen yet?"

"You mean, my theory." He winked.

"Yeah, yeah, sure—your theory."

"Not yet. That's what this is." He reached over his desk and grabbed the file he was writing in. "Was headed there now. Wanna join me?"

"Damn right."

"I'm sure she'll be surprised to see you."

"Maybe. Never know. I'm sure the doc sent over his request for reinstatement."

"Maybe, maybe not. Either way, I'm sure she'll be pissed off as usual to see us." He nudged me and grinned, then led the way directly to Cohen's office.

The walk wasn't far. But when we arrived, she wasn't the only one who waited inside. A man who neither I nor Billy had seen before was sitting behind her desk in the corner. Even in his chair, I could tell he was tall, lanky, and wore cowboy boots and the biggest belt buckle I'd seen in my entire lifetime. The thing needed its own zip code.

Upon entering the room, Billy said, "Who's this?" Without any pleasantries.

"Lyons." Cohen nodded. Then she saw me. A wave of disbelief rushed over her face. Clearly she hadn't received my reinstatement from the doctor. "James? What are you doing here?"

"I've been cleared," I said.

"Seriously?" Confusion lingered.

Billy turned to me and grinned. "That's what I thought." He chuckled at my expense.

I eyed Billy, then Cohen. "Funny. That a problem?" I caught her eye again.

The cowboy sat low in his seat, still refusing to introduce himself. Not until Cohen did it herself. I didn't know why he wouldn't stand up and look us in the eye. Maybe the guy had a hard-on for attention or liked to be called out.

Cohen gestured to the cowboy and said, "This is deputy Jack Kill of the US Marshal Service."

Both Billy and I looked at each other and chuckled. "Deputy Kill? That a joke?" Billy said.

Deputy Kill rose from his seat and stepped toward us. He towered over both Billy and me, easily standing six-foot-four and damned if he wasn't the spitting image of Sam Elliot—both in stature and in cadence. Even the moustache was spot on.

"No joke." He clenched his chiseled jaw and shook both our hands.

I looked down at his hand as he shook mine. It was twice the size, and his grip was stronger than any I'd felt.

"Since this has turned into a manhunt now, the Marshal Service has gotten involved in our search for Mathis. You two will be working side by side with Deputy Kill. Whatever he needs, you supply him with the necessary information. Understood?"

It was bullshit. It's not that I didn't like the Marshal Service, or appreciate the extra help, but if Kill found Mathis before we did, he—no, they—would get to take credit for our capture. I'd be damned if I let that happen.

"Why the sudden burst into my office?" Cohen nodded at the folder in Billy's hand.

"Oh, this?" He looked to it unconsciously.

"Yes. That."

Billy looked to me.

Don't say it. Don't rat me out. Not now. She'll suspend me again.

"I found something while working through the database last night."

I breathed a sigh. *Thank you, Billy.*

"What did you find?" It was the marshal that spoke first, not Cohen.

He opened the manila folder and handed Cohen a copy of the photo I found.

She studied it, then said, "Pretty. Who is she?"

Billy eyed me, like he needed my permission to continue. But I couldn't say or do anything. If I'd truly just been cleared, how could I know that much detail?

But he kept eyeing me. I don't know if he was having a stroke, or if he was simply getting stage freight.

Answer her.

But he didn't.

I had to step in.

"We think . . . she's connected to Mathis somehow."

Cohen didn't even have to think. "I thought you said the doctor just cleared you. How do you know anything about this picture?"

I looked back at Billy. "He brought me up to speed."

"O . . . kay. How is she connected to Mathis?" she said.

"We think she's an ex-lover," I said.

She scrunched her brow. "Why not a sister? Or a friend?"

Seriously? Come on Cohen, you're smarter than that. But I

had to cover my ass, especially since I was just getting back up to speed myself.

"Look at the way she's playing with the camera. She's being frisky with the photographer."

Cohen glanced at the picture one more time before passing it off to Deputy Kill. "She's probably just some model Mathis got a hard-on for," Kill said.

"That's what I . . ." Billy trailed off before he said something he'd regret.

"You what?" Cohen said.

"Nothing," Billy said. "I just mean . . . playing devil's advocate. I wasn't sure, but the more we talked, the more I was convinced."

"So what you're saying here, son, is you think this young woman was Mathis'. . . lover," Kill said. "That sound about right?"

"Ex."

"Sure—ex. But what in the hell does that have to do with this specific case?" Kill said.

"The tattoo." I nodded at the photo he still held.

He studied the photo closer, bringing it to his eye. "OLA?" He gave me a sideways glance, then handed the picture back to Cohen.

"We think the first letter is obscured and it actually reads NOLA," I said.

Then Cohen filled in the rest. "New Orleans, Louisiana."

"That's right," I said.

Cohen gathered herself. She paced the room then spoke. "That's a thin lead, James."

I wasted no time. "What else you got?"

She gritted her teeth. "Take deputy Kill and keep me informed. Up to the second. You got me?" Then she sighed.

"You've got twenty-four hours to chase down this lead. Then I need you back here. Do I make myself clear?"

"Crystal," I said.

Just as we started to leave—me first, then Billy, and finally the deputy, Cohen said, "Deputy."

We all paused.

"Keep them in line, would ya?"

I eyed Billy. We shared a special bond. One that went without saying. He knew what the look meant. We'd ditch the marshal just as soon as we made landfall in the Big Easy.

10

Frozen in shock, Mathis didn't know what to do next. The only thing he could think of was to lower his head and avoid eye contact with any man on the speeding Coast Guard vessel.

"Bastards," he muttered under his breath. He thought the family from the beach had ratted him out. Thought they called the police the moment they set eyes on him.

As the vessel steered closer, it didn't slow down and the captain had to change course to avoid a collision with Mathis and his tiny boat. Mathis came to a dead stop, and the sirens echoed louder as the special purpose vessel sped by him. The wake rocked the boat, and just when the vessel passed, he peered up to see them speed away for open water.

Mathis kept his eyes out to sea, and he didn't spin back around to see what was in front of him until he heard another voice call out.

"Hey. Buddy."

Startled, Mathis quickly found the eye of the one who called for him.

A man sat on a kayak, paddling a pedal-drive contraption with his feet. Two fishing rods were set into the cockpit, ready for deployment at a moment's notice or the first sign of fish on the depth finder the kayak fisherman had installed directly in front of him.

"You get into any fish out there?" the man asked.

Why he thought Mathis was fishing, he didn't know. There wasn't any sign of equipment. No rods. No net. Nothing. The only thing Mathis thought to do was lower his head and shake it. "No. No. No fish."

"Oh well," the man said. "More for me then."

Mathis didn't watch him float past. Again, he avoided eye contact, but found his situation ever more precarious when he saw how many people were around.

A bridge approached. Under it—and just beyond—was the harbor.

The closer he came, the more apparent the difficulty of docking the small vessel on an empty slip became. Mathis released the throttle and allowed the boat to come to a stop again. As the subtle wake lapped on the side of the boat, Mathis stared toward the much larger, more appealing yachts and pontoons cuddled nicely into their boat slips in the marina.

A new plan probed his brain, but before he could act, he looked down at the envelope Cleo had given him before he left. Mathis opened it. There was at least a few hundred dollars inside. He took the money and stuffed the cash inside his pockets, then threw his leg over the starboard side and slid into the cool water. Without being able to dock the vessel, it was time to abandon it and swim for shore.

Mathis was at ease in the water. Before he found himself in trouble with the law, he found himself in trouble with the navy. A lot. After barely graduating high school, he enlisted, aspiring to become a SEAL—because what teenage boy who joins the navy doesn't? But after a few short weeks in BUDs, he rang the bell in defeat. Still though, he had gone through some intense workouts and had always been a good swimmer. He could hold his breath under water for the better part of two minutes.

Mathis dove beneath the surface and flutter kicked his way toward the marina.

He opened his eyes, and the brackish water stung them, but he needed to see. Even if his vision was cloudy. There was a shadow in the water ahead of him. It was a deep hull. Had to be that. Or a massive whale, which didn't seem likely.

The closer he came to the vessel, he realized it was indeed a hull. The vessel was easily over forty feet, maybe bordering on fifty. Mathis surfaced for air along the port side. He pushed himself tight against the fiberglass and swam toward the swim platform.

He bobbed on the water with his arms resting on the transom and searched the area for people. No one was around. Not on the docks, or anywhere close. He listened for talking and as he held his ear out, he saw the name of the yacht etched across the stern.

Lucky Seven.

"Really?" Mathis laughed to himself. "How cliché."

Mathis climbed aboard and skulked along the port side, hugging the gunnel, before entering the cockpit.

He stood at the helm and looked down. The keys were there. "Of course, they are," he said to himself. And why wouldn't they be? As Mathis looked around, he realized the marina was well protected. Gated. No way to get in or out, unless one swam in from the water.

As he stared in wonderment at his own ability to steal an equipped yacht, a man spoke out from the dock. "Hey, Jim. Taking her out today?"

Mathis dropped beneath the helm and hit the deck, knowing the man was talking directly to him. Luckily, there was a plastic sheathing that wrapped around the convertible top. Plus, the windshield protected him from the man's line of sight.

"Jim? You alright up there?" The man was persistent.

Mathis cleared his throat and spoke with a deeper tone. "Ah . . . yeah . . . yeah, just dropped my keys."

He looked around. "Idiot," he said to himself." Then he found the staircase that led to the salon and stateroom. "I've gotta get below deck for a minute."

"Do you mind if I board?" the man said.

"Yes. Don't." Mathis changed his tone without meaning to.

"Oh . . ." the man said.

Mathis could tell he was stunned.

"You sure you alright in there?" the man said.

"Fine. Fine. Just uh . . . not feeling well is all. Got a bit of the stomach flu."

"I see. Well, in that case. Feel better. I'll talk to you tomorrow about our upcoming fishing trip to the Marathon then."

"Yeah, yeah, sure thing, Marathon."

Mathis raised his head above the starboard gunnel and watched the man walk away, then drop into his own boat— a forty-five-foot fishing vessel.

Mathis waited for him to disappear before starting the engine. When the man dropped below deck, Mathis spun the key.

Normally, there was a dockhand to help untie the lines from the dock cleats, but Mathis didn't have that luxury. He leapt for the dock himself and released the tie lines from all four sides, then climbed aboard and returned to the helm. He pulled back on the throttle and started into reverse. There was another vessel in the slip behind him, and backing out would take precision handling to steer out of the marina without causing damage to *Lucky Seven*, or any other boat.

He looked behind him and watched. The yacht handled beautifully. Like pure silk as he spun the helm.

"Jim. Jim," the same man yelled now from the empty slip.

Mathis heard him but didn't spin around. His mind was set on the promise of freedom the boat carried with it.

He looked at the controls and saw the fuel gauge was almost at full. With that amount of fuel, he knew he could get south. How far south depended on his speed. But he could get at least 200 miles away. And for him, that was far enough.

11

The flight from Jacksonville to New Orleans was a little more than an hour. On the plane, Billy and I discussed our approach. We planned to walk around town, see if anyone knew who the woman from the picture. It wasn't much of a plan, but it was the best we had.

"You'd think with all the facial recognition software we have we would've been able to identify this woman," Billy said.

"Obviously, she's done a helluva job staying off the grid," I said.

"Or maybe she's dead," Kill added.

I'd never thought of that option. I eyed him and waited. I knew he had more to add.

"I mean think about it fellas—a man like Mathis ain't gonna keep this picture around because he's sentimental about some fox he used to sleep with. Doesn't add up. Not to me."

"What the hell do you know about it?" Billy said. "You've been on this case for what . . . five minutes?"

"Sounds about right. But I'm not the one who hasn't been able to track him down all these years. That's been y'all's job. A shitty one at that I might add."

"So you think she's dead?" I said.

"Makes sense. Maybe that's why she ain't in your system."

"I don't buy it," I said.

"Me neither," Billy added.

Of course, Billy had my back.

"We shall see, won't we?" Kill said, then turned his attention out the window, as if to say he was done talking to us.

Unconsciously, I did the same just as the wheels touched down on the runway.

THERE WAS a car waiting for us, along with an agent from the New Orleans FBI branch named Micah Duda. He was fresh faced. Looked like he'd just graduated from the academy. I should've figured they'd give us a rookie. No senior agent would have got that detail, especially one that came without a guarantee of capture.

Once we were inside the car, Duda peered in his rearview and asked, "Where to?"

I glanced to Billy. He nodded to let me lead the conversation. Then, I found the marshal's eye.

"Don't look at me, this is y'all's show," Kill said. "I'm just here for the arrest of this fugitive."

"How well do you know this city?" I asked.

"Lived here my whole life."

"That why you got stationed here after the academy?" Billy was quick to say.

"Sure did. Got lucky, I guess. I asked for New Orleans and they gave it to me."

"You asked for it?" I said.

"That's right," Duda said.

"I asked for Washington DC and they put me in Northeast Florida," I turned to Billy and said.

"Me too," Billy said.

"Well, ain't you two cute. Meant to be. Like kismet," Kill said. "Y'all know what that means, don't ya?"

I scrunched my brow and said, "Of course." Even though I didn't.

"You must've done something special at the academy to get your first choice," Billy said.

"Enough already. Stop drooling over the man and tell him what he needs to know," Kill said.

I reached into my pocket and lifted the picture. Worth a try, I figured. "Do you know this woman?"

Duda studied the photo. "No. I saw this pic come through the database. Your team leader sent it over to my boss. He asked me since he knew my history."

"'Cause, you grew up here?" I filled in the blanks.

"No . . ." He paused.

"No? Then why?" I said.

"'Cause, I've worked with some local vice cops on a few cases and he thought the woman may have been a prostitute."

"A prostitute?" I blurted out. Then studied her picture again and scrunched my brow. "No chance."

"That's what I told him, but he insisted."

"What did vice say?" Billy added.

"The two guys I know didn't recognize her. And they know all the working girls in the area."

"So clearly, she's not a hooker," I said. As if I needed to prove it to everyone in the car.

"That's right. So, like I said, where do you wanna go?" Duda said.

I fell back against the back seat. "Start with downtown. Maybe we get lucky."

"Ha." The marshal blurted out. "That sounds about right. The FBI hoping luck will solve their crimes."

I rolled my eyes and sought Billy's attention. He raised his fingers in the shape of a gun, pointed it at the back of the Marshal's seat, and playfully pulled his pretend trigger.

FOR THE BETTER PART OF an hour, we scoured the streets of New Orleans only to come up empty-handed. I honestly didn't know how that was possible. How did no one in the entire city of New Orleans know who she was? It was almost like they were protecting her. Or maybe, she didn't live anywhere near the city. Maybe she just liked the city so much she got it tattooed on her wrist. Or maybe it didn't say NOLA at all? Maybe they were initials of another variety.

I did meet one woman though. For a split second, I could've sworn she recognized the picture, but she couldn't, or wouldn't, say who she was.

When we all regrouped, the others had the look of defeat plastered on their faces.

"Anything?" I asked.

Not one spoke. Just shook their heads no.

"Damnit," I reeled.

But just then, we heard the hideous piercing ring tone of Duda's cell phone. We watched him answer it. "Uh huh, yeah, sure, okay, got it. When?"

We could only hear one end of the conversation, but I was rooted to the spot. He had something.

"She's here now?" Duda said into the phone.

Damn right. I knew it.

"Okay, I'll tell them," Duda said. "Thanks Tony, I owe you one."

When he hung up, I was giddy. Like waiting to open Christmas presents from Santa kind of giddy. "What'd he say?"

"The woman in the picture . . . she's a musician."

I was thrown.

"A musician?" Billy said.

"Yeah, apparently, the photo got around the local precinct. Some detective knew who she was because he had to question her on a case."

"Which case?" I said.

"One that put her brother away for ten years," Duda said.

"No way." I couldn't believe it.

"That's what he tells me," Duda said.

"What's the girl's name?" the marshal asked.

"Cleo Monroe," Duda said.

"Did he say where to find her?" I chimed in.

"*Club Indigo.* It's a lounge."

"Is it close?" I said.

"No more than a few blocks."

Billy reached out and smacked me on the ass. "Good work, James."

Kill saw Billy's gesture, and turned a weird eye to me, then said, "You touch me like that Agent Lyons, and I'll deck you where you stand."

"Wouldn't dream of it." Billy eyed the marshal and winked.

I chuckled, then followed Duda, trying to figure out the story I was going to pitch when I met the beautiful stranger from the picture.

12

WE WALKED TO THE BAR. STANDING OUT FRONT, I REACHED for the door. I was expecting it to be locked—especially at the morning hour—but it wasn't.

Duda walked through the opening and said, "Some places down here don't know the meaning of closing time."

Billy followed Duda, then the marshal, who looked at me and said, "Drunken fools."

I grinned, but mainly to appease him.

Inside, a man stood behind the wood bar, wiping it with a dish rag. He saw us and said, "Sorry, but I don't serve until ten. From the looks of you four though, I don't imagine this is a social call."

Are we that obvious? Maybe that's why we didn't get very far with the people on the street.

"No. It's not," I was the first to say. I figured if this was my idea, then I should be the one to lead the conversation. "We're looking for a young woman. A woman named Cleo Monroe."

The bartender nodded up and down. "She played here a

few nights back. Helluva jazz musician. And a beauty at that."

"Do you know where we might be able to find her?"

The bartender eyed us.

"She in some kind of trouble?" he said.

"No . . . no." I held up my hand to deflect his defensive tone. "Nothing like that. We just need to ask her a few questions, that's all."

I watched the bartender bite down hard and clench his jaw. It was easy to tell he had information. But was going to tell us?

"You got a warrant?"

"Obviously not or we wouldn't be here right now," Billy said.

I shot him a sour glare. Then returned my attention on the bartender. "No, sir. Like I said, we were hoping to ask her a few questions."

"What about?"

"I'm afraid that's classified information," I said.

I expected him to turn more defensive after I fed him a line of bureaucratic nonsense. But it was truth.

"It ain't about that guy she was with, was it?"

"Guy?" I looked to Billy. A questioning look hung on his face as it did mine. Did we have him? Was it Mathis? Did he come to see her? "What guy?"

"Uh . . ." The bartender stalled, then threw his rag over his shoulder and wiped his hands together to dry them.

"Wait." I held up my hand and cut him off. Then reached into my pocket for the picture I carried of Mathis. "Was this the man?"

The bartender eyed it for a second, then brought it closer for focus.

In actuality, the picture was old, but still resembled Mathis.

"Yeah. Yeah, I think so."

I slapped Billy on the shoulder and grinned from ear to ear.

"Honestly though, I can't be certain," the bartender added.

Then Kill stepped forward with his phone. "How 'bout this? He look more familiar now?"

"Yeah. Yeah. That's the guy. Definitely." The bartender pointed directly at the phone.

Kill sneered as he turned and looked me square in the eye. "Bring the man an outdated picture." He shook his head from side to side. "Classic FBI move."

Before I could even respond to Kill's dig at me and the FBI, the bartender spoke again. "He came in near the end of her set. Then waited around until she finished. They left together."

"When? What time?" I asked.

The bartender looked up and left to recall. "Two. a.m. Like I said, it was a few nights back."

"But you still remember her?" Billy said.

"Oh yeah, of course. She's a native here. Aside from being a talented musician, she's a patron as well."

"Does she come often?" I said.

"Hasn't since that night. You don't think that sicko did something to her, do you?"

"No. No. That's not likely," I said. Although Mathis had done something out of the norm when he shot me.

"That's why we want to find her. Make sure she's alright," Billy said.

Perfect pitch. I could always rely on Billy to say the right thing at the right time. From his protective tone, I assumed the bartender had a thing for her.

It didn't take more than a second for him to tell us where she lived. Said he had to put her in a cab on more than one occasion. Too drunk to find her way home.

"Is that close?" I asked him, but it was Duda who answered my question.

"It's not far at all," he said.

"Thank you, sir. You've been a tremendous help. If you think of anything else, or you see this man again, you call this number." I handed him my business card and followed everyone outside back into the bright sun.

"We gonna walk? Or drive?" Billy asked Duda.

"We'll drive."

"I hate to be the one to say this, but . . ." Kill started. "What if Mathis is holed up at this Ms. Cleo's house? Waiting for us?"

"Waiting for us?" I was surprised Kill's mind went there.

"Y'all said he did something out of the ordinary by shooting you in the chest—all I'm saying is . . . what if he's there? Don't you think we should alert the cavalry? Or do you want to end up shot again?"

Of course the marshal would take yet another dig at me. I guess I was easy pickin's. Without thinking, I looked toward my chest and felt where the bullets would've hit.

"The old man has a point," Billy said.

"Who you calling old man?" Kill growled.

"Well . . ." Billy looked him over. "You."

I stepped in between them before Billy started a fight with a man nearly thirty years his senior. Not because I thought that Billy would knock him out or send him to the hospital, but rather for his own benefit. Kill was in incredible shape and must've had old man strength. Maybe even something superhuman to still be doing the job at his age.

"Easy, fellas. Let's just take this slow. I say we check on the property. Surveil her for a couple hours. Maybe follow her if she leaves the premises. That way, we can stop and ask her questions away from home. Just in case she is hiding him. Sound good?" I said.

Each man nodded in agreement, and we followed Duda back to the car for yet another adventure.

13

IN THE BACKSEAT OF THE SEDAN, I WAS SWEATING. DUDA CUT the engine because we didn't want to waste gas by sitting in idle. But even with the windows down it was hot. Damn hot. Hotter than Florida when we left. I couldn't believe the humidity. It had to be pushing ninety percent and there wasn't a breath of wind.

We were only in the car for about fifteen minutes before we caught our first glimpse of Cleo.

"There." I pointed.

I was the first to see her. Maybe I was paying the closest attention.

She came out wearing form fitting shorts and a sports bra with matching Nike tennis shoes. She turned to the left and right before reaching for her ear buds. After putting them inside her ears, she turned away from us and started into a brisk jog.

"What now? Do we go after her?" Duda asked.

"Not much of a runner, are you, kid?" Kill said.

"No. Why?"

"Because eventually, she's gotta come back," Billy filled in the blank.

Kill looked over his shoulder from the front seat and eyed Billy. "I guess the FBI does teach some common sense."

"Only a little," Billy snapped back.

"Right, but how far is she gonna run?" Duda said.

Billy leaned near to me and watched her go. "She looks like she's in pretty good shape. I'd say we got at least twenty minutes."

"Really? I was thinking fifteen," Kill said.

But I was done wasting time. I reached for the handle and pulled.

"What the hell are you doing?" Billy said.

"What's it look like? The first sign of that bastard and I'm busting that door down." I jumped out of the backseat and stared down the road. A car was coming, and I waited to cross.

When I reached the sidewalk, I heard Billy from over my shoulder. "I'm not letting you get shot again. The boys will wait for our signal. If we need them, I'll radio back."

I grinned and we both continued toward Cleo's address. "Just another Saturday, huh, Billy?"

"Damn right."

Billy stood by her front door and peered inside. I took the side entrance. The house was a newly renovated cottage style home with a concrete patio that led up to the red door. There were lots of windows to let the light in, but they were covered by gossamer curtains. Even the front door had frosted glass.

As I walked along the side of the home, I saw four

windows. I leaned on my tiptoes and looked inside the first one I came to. There was a couch and a loveseat facing the corner where there had to be a TV, I couldn't tell from my position.

The next window was small and completely blacked out —a bathroom.

As I crept closer to the back of the home, I came to another. This one was bigger. Two side by side windows with the curtains slightly pulled back. As I looked, I saw movement. My heart raced. Something was on the floor. I took another step and my heart began to pound inside my chest. I reached for my FBI-issued-Glock 23 and lifted it free from the holster.

I couldn't control my breathing. I should've called Billy, but I couldn't—not in that moment. I had to react to the movement. But before I could, a loud screeched banged against the wall. I jumped in freight only to see a tabby cat dart across the bedroom floor.

"Excuse me," I heard a woman's voice call out from behind and back toward the front where Billy stood.

That had to be Cleo. I holstered my Glock and spun around to follow the call. I jogged the length of the cottage and found Cleo waiting for an explanation.

"Who are you? Why are you on my doorstep?" she said.

"Calm down, ma'am."

I watched Billy turn his body to the side. Get her to realize he wasn't a threat. Standard procedure.

When Billy caught my eye, she turned around to see me standing behind her.

"And who the hell is this?" She threw her arms in disgust.

She was upset we'd come to see her. Which could only mean one thing: she had something to hide.

"I know my rights." She started with the cliched response.

"We understand that, ma'am. We're not trying to impugn upon those rights, we simply want to ask you a few questions."

"About what?"

I was standing next to Billy then.

"A man named Archibald Mathis," I said.

"Never heard of him," she didn't even think about it.

"Are you sure about that?" I said.

"I think so. I'm pretty good with names. Now if you don't mind, I'd like to get in my home and get into the shower, I'm gonna be late."

She stepped in between us and we parted. But before she could reach the door handle, I spoke again. "Because a certain bartender at *Club Indigo* happened to tell us you and Mr. Mathis seemed pretty chummy after your gig a few nights back."

"Chummy?" Billy muttered. "Who says, chummy?"

We watched her head fall. She was still showing us her back.

"Look, ma'am, we can get a federal warrant and search your property and bring you in for questioning. Then once we find out more you'll likely be charged with aiding and abetting a fugitive, and maybe accessory after the fact . . . you know the list goes on and on. But why not avoid that hassle and just tell us where he is?" I said.

When she finally raised her head, she spoke through tears. "I don't know where he is."

"Let's start with what you do know," Billy said.

She turned around. The tears that fell didn't mask the pain in her eyes. She cared for him. That much was easy to see.

"We understand. He means something to you. You don't know him like we know him," I tried to empathize with her.

"Or maybe you do," Billy added.

I glanced Billy's way, but didn't let his comment linger in her mind. Her head dropped again, and she tried to suck back the tears.

It was time to give it straight. "He shot me."

Those words sent her upright, and she held her breath.

"Two slugs. Right here." I pointed to my chest. "If I wasn't wearing a bullet-proof vest, I'd be dead."

I let those words sink in and didn't speak again until she was ready to do so.

"He's not a . . ." she said in between sobs, "violent man."

"We know. He's just a thief who took his freedom too far. He didn't want to get caught and put away for the rest of his natural born life," Billy said.

She swallowed the lump in her throat, then spoke again. "I . . . I . . . let him have a boat."

"Where?"

"South of the city. It was at my friend's property . . . Please they aren't a part of this. Please don't violate their home."

"We'll do our best to limit the damage," I said. "Can you take us there?"

Stuffing back more tears, she nodded up and down. "Can I call them to tell them we're coming?"

"Please do. Explain to them that we would be happy with their cooperation."

She bit her lower lip. I could tell there was more.

"What is it?"

"They don't like the government much."

"Not many people down this way do, ma'am," Billy said.

"Like I said. We would be grateful for their cooperation. And you can tell them, we won't file charges against them for obstruction of justice."

She nodded, then said, "Give me a few minutes to shower off. Then I'll be out."

She turned and walked to her door again, but before she stepped inside, Billy said, "We've got two more men. We'll be stationed around your house, so don't go thinking your gonna run on us."

She peered over her shoulder and said, "Wouldn't dream of it."

After going inside, Billy lifted his radio and called, "We got 'em. Caught a ride on a boat. Come to the house for support. She'll be out in a few minutes to take us to the launch site. Over."

"Roger that. Over."

When Billy dropped the radio to his side, he said, "You still think he's anywhere near here?"

"Nope."

"Really? Why?"

"Depending on the size of the boat Cleo gave him, I can't imagine he got very far. He either headed up the Mississippi or down into the Gulf."

"What's your bet?" Billy said.

"The Gulf."

"Really? Back to Florida?"

"That's what I'd do. Come into the panhandle and steal something bigger. Try to get as far south as I could. Mexico. Costa Rica, maybe. Somewhere in Central America."

74

"Better call Cohen then. Tell her to get the Coast Guard on the line," Billy said.

"Already on it." I showed him my phone was already dialing.

14

On the road from New Orleans, I couldn't help but notice the surrounding beauty of the passing flora and fauna. As we passed the first of many swamps, there was a congregation of egrets hovering above, searching the water below for a quick meal.

"Deer." Kill yelled.

I whipped my head around in time to see a buck standing just off the shoulder. But he didn't stay. As soon as the deer felt the presence of our car, he scampered deep into the brush.

"Thank the Lord Bambi didn't sprint into the road," Kill said in between deep breaths.

"Bambi was a girl," Duda said.

"No, Bambi was a boy," Kill looked over at him and said.

"Yeah. Don't you remember the antlers?" Billy said.

Duda sat silent, then said, "Really? Bambi was a boy?"

"Yep," Kill said.

"How could I think he was a girl?" Duda muttered under his breath.

"It's the name. Throws people off," Billy said.

I went back to looking out the window and noticed a hawk gliding in the sky. I loved hawks. Truth was, I was a bit of a bird lover—always had been. My dad was an ornithologist by trade. His favorite raptor was the bald eagle. I remember him going all over the world to study birds. When I was young, he even took me to some pretty crazy locales.

Nostalgia got the better of me as I searched the sky above for more swooping predators, I didn't even hear Kill ask me the question. Not until Billy hit me on the shoulder.

"What?" I stared at him.

"I said, what's with Mathis?" Kill said.

I found his eye and said, "What do you mean?"

"I mean, how has he eluded y'all?" Kill said.

Words got stuck in my mouth. I wanted to tell him why, but most of what I thought was either an excuse or a bold face lie.

"According to his sheet, he was into some petty stuff when he was younger. Larceny, right? Robbing friends of their jewelry and such? But then moved heavier scores by robbing a couple banks. I heard some jewelry stores in Georgia and Louisiana. Even grabbed one in Florida. Then there was the famous heist—the one where you messed up with the armored truck in Kentucky."

"We didn't mess up. Local PD botched the crime scene," Billy said.

But that wasn't true. It was me. I messed up. Billy had always done a great job of protecting me.

Kill continued, "So how did he escape you this time? How did you end up with two slugs in the chest?"

Kill was staring at me. Duda too—through the rearview

mirror. And Billy. The question felt like an interrogation, and I started to sweat. The sweat beaded at my hairline and drenched my armpits. I didn't know why, but Kill was one of those intimidating men. You know the type: a man who could make you feel uncomfortable to the point of spilling your deepest, darkest secrets without intending to.

"We got a tip that someone saw a man fitting his description near the Jacksonville airport. Naturally that tip came across the wire. I wasn't there, but—"

"—I was," Billy interrupted.

"How long had it been since the last sighting?" Kill said.

"Almost a year," I said.

"A year?" Kill's voice went deeper, then higher.

"Yeah. We followed a few other leads throughout the country, even one outside. Went down to Mexico—near Playa Del Carmen—but each lead turned out to be a complete bust. If he was in any of those places, he was long gone by the time we got there. That's when I got the call from Billy. I just happened to be on my way back down to the Jacksonville office from Atlanta."

"I was still up in Atlanta on an assignment," Billy said.

"And I was barely over the Florida-Georgia line when he said—"

"—I told him I'd be on a plane as soon as I could, but . . ." Billy said.

"—I knew there wouldn't be time. So, I tracked the lead down by myself."

"Why didn't you alert local PD?" Kill said.

"And have them screw it up again?" Billy said.

I put my hand out to ease Billy's rising heartrate and blood pressure. "We didn't want to have everyone coming in hot. Sirens blaring. That would draw too much attention. Mathis was too smart for that."

"What then?" Kill said.

"I found him."

"Where?" Kill said.

"At the airport. He was waiting to board and next in line by the ticketing agent. By luck, he happened to turn and see me before I could get close. Then he ran down the jet bridge and stormed out the door. You know the one that is at the end of the jet bridge before you board the plane?"

"Sure," Kill said.

"He commandeered one of the luggage loading machines and drove off. By the time I got to him, he'd found a worker's truck and boosted it. I tracked him all the way to Jacksonville Port Authority before he took out his gun and shot me twice."

"Holy shit, that's intense," Duda said.

"You're telling me," I said.

"Why didn't you shoot first?" Kill said.

"I didn't know he was armed. I had my gun on him, but before I knew what was happening, he put two into my chest."

"Sounds like you hesitated," Kill said.

"I didn't hesitate." I clenched my jaw and stared right through him. But he didn't respond. He just looked at me knowingly, then turned around.

He was facing forward when he said, "You sure about that?"

Wait? Did I? My mouth stayed open as I pondered.

Then Duda said, "Looks like we're here."

The car rolled to a stop, and I eyed Billy. He grinned but

didn't say anything. And I didn't open the door until all three men were outside waiting for me to get out.

How could I? Why would I have hesitated? But I wouldn't find my answer there. Not alone in the back of the car. Not until I tracked Mathis down and put him away. Only then would the itch of hesitating go away.

15

Stepping out into the hot sun, I saw two people standing in front of a battered shack waiting to meet us. The woman looked very athletic, as did the man. They must have been bodybuilders. By the looks on their square-jawed faces, they were not happy to see us.

Cleo walked over to greet them before any of us stepped away from our car. She turned and nodded before I made the first move. Not that we needed her permission, it was just what she requested before we left New Orleans.

The closer I walked toward the man and woman, the bigger they became. When I finally stopped in front of them, the man stood over me by four inches and had me by at least 100 pounds. I wasn't small either. I stood six feet tall and weighed about 190 pounds.

I gulped, then asked, "Did Cleo tell you why we're here?"

They both nodded but didn't offer a response. Only a judgmental stare.

"Cleo tells us Mr. Mathis escaped through your backyard, is that correct?"

Again, they nodded yes.

"Would you mind showing us where?" Billy added.

They looked to him, then turned and walked around the side of the home. I eyed Billy. My eyes bulged as I nodded to the backs of them. The concern in Billy's eyes mirrored my own. The couple could be a significant threat if it came down to it.

Behind their home was a bayou, and the marshy ground squished beneath my feet. There hadn't been a hurricane or saturating rain in some time, so I was surprised to see the water pooling around my feet.

Ahead was a boat shed with two slips. One was empty. The other full with an airboat tied up.

"This where he take off from?" Kill said.

The big man nodded.

"In what type of boat?" I had to ask an open-ended question to elicit a response.

"Wood skiff," the big man muttered in an accent I could barely understand.

"Motor?" Kill asked.

The big man nodded and said, "A tiller steer."

"How big?" I asked.

He spoke again, but this time I couldn't even decipher what he said.

"I see," Kill said. Apparently, he could.

"Come again?" I said.

"Nine horse," Kill spoke out the side of his mouth.

That was small. But on a full tank, he could still get far enough away. Especially if he hugged the coastline or headed up the Mississippi River.

"Any idea which way he went?" I said.

The big man pointed southeast.

"Thank you, sir," I said.

The four of us broke away from Mr. and Mrs. Universe for a moment and moved toward the airboat. The waterline of the bayou was high, nearly cascading over the edge of the property.

I searched the swamp and didn't say anything to the others as the three of them made conversation behind me. If I were Mathis, where would I have gone? The breeze picked up and kissed my cheek as I watched the water ripple on the surface. In the distance, an alligator dipped below the surface and thrashed its tail before spinning off and traveled deeper into the swamp. The breeze was a welcome sensation on my skin, even if it was only for a moment.

I didn't see Billy sneaking up behind me. "What you thinking?" he whispered.

I looked over my shoulder. "I say we take this airboat and scavenge the area. See what we can find."

"You think we call it in? Use the New Orleans field office for backup? I know that Kill is itching to call in reinforcements with the marshal's service. Thinks he's gonna be the one to track Mathis down."

I spun around. "Let him call his boys. They won't be here in time. Not after we get a head start in the airboat."

"You think Captain America will let us use this?" Billy kicked the side.

"I've got an ace up my sleeve," I said, then stepped passed Billy and walked back toward the disturbed couple.

"An ace?" Billy jumped in behind me and tried to keep up.

The enormous couple didn't break their stare as I walked toward them. But as intimidating as they were, I didn't waver. "We need to take your airboat."

"Excuse me?" the woman said. "Absolutely not. We allowed you on our property out of respect for Cleo, but don't think for one second we're going to willingly let you take our property."

"Well I could have the marshal here seize your property." I turned to open my hand toward Kill.

"Excuse me?" the woman was adamant with her body language and syllables. "I don't think so."

"No?" I questioned. "Why else do you think we've come?"

I looked to Billy, then the marshal, and finally Duda. All wore questioning looks. None knew I'd made a call when we found our destination. Turned out the monster and his bride were into some illegal dealings.

The woman was silent. Then she said, "What do you mean? Why you've come?"

"I know you and your husband have been running an illegal enterprise out of this property for some time now. The US Marshal Service has asked us to try to bargain with you. If you are unwilling to work with us on our investigation, they're only a phone call away." I took out my phone and flipped it toward them. "I can give this to Mr. Kill, and he can make the call to freeze your assets and forfeit your home."

The woman looked to her husband. The harshness dropped from their brows, and then fear crossed their faces.

"So like I said. We need your boat."

The big man pointed. "Keys inside."

"Thank you," I said, then turned around and walked toward it.

Billy followed close behind me, then leaned into my ear and whispered, "That was amazing. That wasn't an ace, that was damn royal flush."

We shared a chuckle before jumping aboard the airboat. I sat in the pilot's chair, and the others sat in the bench seat in front of me.

I grabbed the stick to my left and felt it. The handle hugged my hand. And as I grasped it, memories from my youth rushed back. I said my father was an ornithologist, but I neglected to mention I spent some of my youth on my mother's side. She was from Louisiana. Not New Orleans, but close enough to be familiar with the inner workings of an airboat.

"Do you know how to drive this thing?" Duda asked.

"Can't be that hard." I was messing with him.

"I'm not good on boats," Duda said. "Get sick sometimes."

"Great," Kill said.

"Here switch with me," Billy moved so Duda could sit along the gunnel. "You gotta puke, do it that way." He pointed to the port side.

"Ready?" I said.

"Hit it." Billy seemed to be the only one excited.

"Don't forget to put your earmuffs on." There was a collection of them on the floor. "'Cause this is gonna be loud."

I started the fan and backed away into the swampy unknown, searching for a man who could be anywhere.

16

TO MY SURPRISE, THERE WERE OTHERS WHO JOINED THE HUNT. We didn't get five minutes away from the property before three other boats met us in the middle of the bayou. When they came close, Kill spun around and offered a smile.

"Damn marshals," I said loud, but nobody heard me through the howling wind of the air boat.

Travel through the swamps was slow going. There were multiple downed trees in the water. I hit one, maybe two. My captaining skills weren't as sharp as they used to be. It had been years since I last piloted an airboat.

Hovering over the banks of the bayou, I scanned for any sign of an abandoned wood skiff. There was nothing. The search was a complete waste of our time. Mathis wasn't hiding in the trees like Wesley Snipes in *U.S. Marshals*—a great movie by the way—he was gone. Long gone. Deep into the Gulf of Mexico.

I steered the airboat onto the shoreline of someone's property and cut off the fan.

"You see something?" Billy ripped his headphones off.

"No. Nothing," I said.

"Then why are we stopping?" Kill said.

Another boat followed us onto land and two men in US Marshal jackets jumped from the bow of their airboat. They puffed up their chests and searched the grounds incessantly, like they saw something. But I knew better.

"There's nothing there. Mathis is gone."

"Where is he?" Duda said.

I thought for a moment. Then said, "Put out the word along the Alabama coast and the panhandle of Florida. Contact local PD. See if there's been any abandoned boat sightings. Guarantee someone has seen something."

"How do you know he went into the Gulf?" Kill said.

"Because I know Mathis. He's not gonna head upriver. It's too risky. It's narrow in spots and he's more likely to be seen. In the Gulf, he can disappear if he wants to."

"That may be true, but he's in a small boat. If he went out to sea, that's a death sentence," Kill said. "With the fuel capacity of the motor, he'd need to stay along the coastline, where he'd also risk being seen."

"True, but less of a risk. And he knows the ocean. Knows how to read the tides. He can blend in easier, trust me. Just make the call."

The two marshals who stood on shore looked to Kill for an order. One said, "What's your call, sir?"

Kill huffed. I could tell he didn't want to listen to me. "Do what he says. See what you can find," he said.

"Yes, sir." The man lifted his phone.

I nodded to Kill, but he gave me a sour glare before jumping off the airboat himself.

After turning my attention to Duda, I said, "Call it in. See if you can crosscheck that info with what we know."

"Roger that." He leaped over the bow.

Billy looked to me, then stepped over the bench seat. "Let's make a bet."

Whenever Billy started a conversation like that, he was reluctant to believe me. At least, that was the way it had always been in the past. "Okay, what's the bet?"

"The usual amount . . . twenty."

"Sure, twenty," I said. "But what are we betting on?"

"Where the skiff was found, and whether Mathis was in it."

"For my sake, I hope he wasn't found. I need to collar that bastard myself."

"I know that's what you want, but is that realistic?"

Mathis was far from us, and the trail had gone cold, at least it had until the lead with Cleo. But if we were going to bet, at least I was going to set the terms. "The boat's in Mobile. The farthest, Pensacola."

"You think?"

"It would make sense with the fuel capacity of the motor. Besides, if he was found, I'm sure we would've heard something by now."

"You're right. No way Cohen would let us to chase our tails . . ." Billy paused. "Or maybe she would, just to piss us off." He winked and nudged me. "So, you wanna head to Mobile?"

"Let's wait to see what Duda and Kill come up with."

Billy turned and was about to step over the seat and make his own way to shore, but before he did, I asked. "Wait."

He spun around.

"What's your guess?" I said.

"Lost at sea."

"Really? You think?"

"No, but I figure I let you win this one. You know, considering you took two shots to the chest for him." He chuckled to himself then jumped on shore.

"Funny guy, aren't you?" I yelled as he walked away.

Kill had a look on his face, like he had some critical information. Like he wanted to say something, but if he did, I'd be proven right.

"They found something," he said.

That stopped Billy in his tracks.

"Who found something?" I said.

"Local sheriff found a boat. Unoccupied and drifting in the harbor," Kill said.

"Where?" I said.

"There's more," he said.

I stepped down from the piloting chair and walked toward him.

"How much more?"

"A man in that same harbor called the sheriff about a strange man posing as his friend and a local boat owner."

"Mathis," I muttered.

Kill continued, "Apparently, the man who called in said this stranger was pretending to be sick or something. Staying out of view but answering his questions. Naturally, he was suspicious and called 911, but not before the stranger stole the yacht and headed out to sea."

"You're kidding," Billy said.

"I'm not," Kill said.

"Did they get a positive ID on Mathis?"

Kill stalled, then said, "No."

"Damnit." I reeled.

"But the sheriff did snap a photo of the abandoned boat.

They're sending me a picture soon. If we bring the photo back to the big guy and his wife, we can have them verify if this was the boat they gave Mathis," Kill said.

"Where was the boat found?" I said.

"Near Orange Beach and Perdido Key."

I found Billy's eye and grinned. "The Florida-Alabama border."

"Looks like you were right," Billy said.

"And you owe me twenty bucks."

Billy felt for his shirt, then shoved his hands in his pocket and turned them out and shrugged. "Looks like I'll have to owe you."

"Figures."

17

MR. AND MRS. BEEFCAKE PROVIDED US WITH A POSITIVE ID of the boat. Mathis *was* in Perdido Key. And even though our 911 caller didn't get a visual on Mathis, it couldn't have been a coincidence. Especially when we got the specs on the vessel Mathis stole. A yacht aptly named *Lucky Seven* with enough fuel capacity to get him away from Pensacola. Which made our search area a helluva lot bigger.

I didn't know if Mathis was smart enough to disconnect the GPS location device on the yacht, but I imagined he was. My theory was confirmed when the coast guard pinged the GPS only to come back empty.

But in doing so, he'd be navigating blind—something only a seasoned sailor should try. Was Mathis that good? I didn't really know. All I knew was I sure as hell wouldn't be —and I'd been around boats my entire life.

Pulling into the marina near Perdido Key, I saw a man surrounded by two officers dressed in uniforms. One looked like the local sheriff, the other his deputy.

"Is that our guy?" Billy said.

Billy and I rode together now that we split off from Duda. He stayed in New Orleans, though he'd assured us he would be on the next plane out if we needed his help. A sweet offer, but we didn't need him.

Kill drove in behind us in his own sedan. He was accompanied by another marshal—one from the airboat search team. Just what we needed, more marshals.

"Looks like it." I shoved the car into park.

We jumped out and made our way toward the marina. As we came upon the sheriff, the other man in uniform spun around and saw us first. I watched him tap the sheriff on the arm and gesture that we were approaching. The sheriff muttered something—I could see his mouth move—but couldn't make out what he said. Guarantee it was a something curt about the FBI.

"Ah, the feds are here." The sheriff folded his arms and covered his notes.

I didn't know why he held such contempt for us. We'd never met the man. Maybe he had an axe to grind. Or maybe he just had little man syndrome.

I towered over him. He couldn't have been more than five foot four.

"Just what in the Sam Hill can we do for you fella's?" the sheriff asked in a southern drawl.

Broxton, his name tag said. "Sheriff Broxton, I'm Agent James. This is Agent Lyons. Is that the eyewitness?" I motioned over his shoulder as he and the deputy blocked him off.

"It is."

I stalled for a moment, wondering why Broxton hadn't stepped aside so we could do our jobs. By the time I was about to speak again, Kill and the other marshal caught up to us.

"Could you please step aside, sir so we can ask him a few questions?" I said.

"I could, sure . . . but will I . . . ?" Broxton said.

I looked to Billy. *What the hell is with this guy? Is he trying to be cute or just an asshole?*

"We don't have time for this pissing contest. Get out of the way." Kill pushed Broxton aside with little effort and led the witness into the open gate of the harbor.

"Excuse me." I stepped around Broxton and his deputy and followed Kill and the witness.

Broxton continued to stand with his arms folded as we walked around.

As we moved away, Billy leaned into me and asked, "What's with that guy?"

"No idea."

But as we continued, we got our answer. "Still waiting to hear on my application. It's been a year already," Broxton yelled.

Both of us stopped and stood in awe.

"Obviously, he's still holding out hope," Billy spoke out of the side of his mouth to me. Then he yelled back. "Yeah, we're backed up right now. Keep waiting. Sometimes it can take up to four or five years to hear back."

"You're such a dick," I chuckled and muttered.

Poor guy did have an axe to grind; he'd been holding out hope for far too long.

"That's what I figured," Broxton played off the comment.

When we caught up with the marshals and the witness, the three of them stopped in front of an empty slip. We arrived in time to hear the witness offer his name. "Mike

Love." Then he said, "This is where the boat was stolen from."

All of us looked to the open slip.

"How do you know it wasn't the owner who took the boat out?" Billy was playing the critic.

"Because Jim Peoples is my friend. He was out of town on business—which is why I approached the boat in the first place when I saw someone aboard. I wanted to see if he was back early or if something happened."

"So what did the man say?" Kill said.

"I asked if I could come board. He made up some excuse about needing to go below deck. Then suddenly he got sick."

"Sick?" I said.

"Yeah, sick. I didn't buy that, so I made up a story," Love said.

"You did? What story?" I said.

"About going on a fishing trip together. I baited him."

"Smart," Billy added.

"I said we were planning a trip to fish at Marathon together. Truth is Jim hates to fish. Dive sure, but fishing . . . he can't stand the smell."

"What then?" I said.

"I went to call the police. I didn't want him to hear me, so I disappeared for a minute. That's when I saw the boat start to pull away. I ran to the pier again and shouted Jim's name."

"And you still couldn't identify the person aboard?" Kill said.

"No, not really."

Even though it was a long shot, I needed to ask. I pulled out Mathis' photo and said, "Was this the man?"

He looked at, then shrugged. "I don't know, could be."

Damnit Mathis, where are you? But as I searched the harbor, I knew there was only one possible exit—the Gulf of Mexico. I bit my lip and dropped my shoulders, then found the entrance of the harbor—back where the sheriff and his deputy stood. "Thank you for your time, Mr. Love." I shook his hand and walked away.

Billy caught me and said, "What do you think? How far do you think he could've gone?"

"A yacht that size? With a full tank?" I said.

Billy nodded yes.

I let the wind out of my lungs and shrugged. "Who knows? Two—three hundred miles?"

The number stopped Billy in his tracks. Not that he hadn't expected me to say it, but maybe it hit him hard. And the fact we would have to relay this information to Cohen would be that much harder. But hey, at least we had some leads.

A big van with ACTION NEWS 20 written on the side, steered into the parking lot of the marina. Word had begun to spread.

I watched as Sheriff Broxton whispered to his deputy. The lanky deputy departed from Broxton's side and ran toward the racing vehicles to cut off their approach.

"Hey, Sheriff," I said as I walked up.

He saw me coming but spun back around, annoyed. "What can I help you with now, *Hoover*?"

"Don't be a dick," I retorted. I called him out and instantly he let his guard down.

"I'm sorry, it's just . . . you know . . . it's been my life's dream to be an FBI agent. I know I'd be great. Out in the trenches with you guys, chasing down bad guys. Does it get any better than that?"

"I know you would be," I said.

"You really think so? You think I've got what it takes?"

"Oh, yeah. Hell, I'd be your partner." The FBI didn't have partners. At least not in the capacity he was thinking.

His eyes lit up, and his face softened. Then he lowered his head bashfully.

"Where did you find the boat?" I said.

"I thought . . ." He motioned over my shoulder. I turned and saw Billy coming up the pier. "Mr. Love would've told you that."

"Not that boat, Sheriff. The abandoned skiff."

"Oh, she's in the local impound lot now."

"Can you show me where?" I said just as Billy joined me by my side.

"On one condition," he whispered.

"What's that?" I whispered back.

"You leave Wyatt Earp behind." He pointed directly at Kill.

I followed the sheriff's arm, then looked to Billy. "With pleasure."

"Good. Then follow me."

18

THE WIND SWEPT THROUGH MATHIS'S HAIR AS HE STOOD AT the helm. There was nothing but ocean blue in front of him. Orange Beach was in his rearview, and the threat of the FBI seemed like a distant memory. Mathis smiled. If only for a moment, it felt like he was captaining his own vessel. Taking it out for a pleasure cruise. Maybe on a dive in the gulf or on some fishing expedition. It didn't matter. All that mattered in that moment was that he felt free.

He set course for Clearwater—the first stop of many on his new adventure. Staying along the Florida border was his only choice. At the crushing speed of seventeen knots, he didn't have the fuel capacity to make it much farther before needing to refuel. But with the stolen yacht and his face plastered all over the television, the question was . . . could he keep his identity hidden when the time came to interact with people?

HE EASED up on the throttle, pulled it into neutral position, and stared toward the shoreline through a pair of binoculars. He was one nautical mile offshore but unaware of his exact location. There was a map laid out beneath him. He glanced to it, and then back at the beach. If his compassing skills were up to snuff, he was confident he was close to Clearwater Beach.

As he continued searching through the lenses, he scanned to the south. There was a break there—an inlet that separated the north side of the beach and the south side. He couldn't remember many other peninsulas that looked similar along the Gulf Coast—at least not in the direct vicinity of Clearwater Beach.

After visiting Clearwater only once in his life, he remembered there was a marina with a refueling station inside the inlet.

Mathis set his binoculars down and pushed the throttle forward, steering toward the inlet. He kept his wake at a minimum. As he travelled, small kids gathered and began to wave at him from the beach off his port side. No way they could recognize his face, but still, he kept his eyes away and concentrated on the task.

Ahead was a bridge with enough clearance for him to pass under. He breathed a sigh, knowing if it wasn't, he would have had to alert the drawbridge master to raise it.

Squawking sea gulls flying overhead made him turn his eye to the sky, and in the moment of distraction, another vessel approached—a sailboat. He didn't see it, not until one short blast of his horn brought Mathis back down to earth to avoid a head on collision.

His heart pounded in his chest. He swerved to the right and clearly caught disdain from the passing sailboat captain.

Again, Mathis kept his head down in fear of being identified.

Once under the bridge, Mathis steered north and around the point. There was another skinny inlet that he had to pass through. At low tide, the hull of the yacht might have been close to scraping the bottom, but at high tide there was plenty of clearance.

Off the bow, there were three veined offshoots, each with homes built along the water to take full advantage of their bay views. Farther north was another roadway. He didn't pay much attention there, because at the far end—on the other side of the rows of homes—was the harbor. It was stocked full of boats, but there was an empty slip—a refueling station—precisely where Mathis would dock the vessel.

A few dockhands were scattered around the area, tending to other customers. Steering the vessel close, Mathis didn't wait for the dockhand to wave him in, so he took it upon himself to dock the yacht himself. Not something easily done without expert handling skills.

As Mathis lined himself up with the pier, a man walked out and began waving his arms, trying to get his attention at the helm. Mathis paid him no mind. He just continued. The man stopped waving his arms, then guided him into the slip.

Once docked, Mathis walked to the transom where the dockhand was waiting for him. Before Mathis could ask him to refuel, the dockhand spoke instead, "Y'all looking for fuel?"

"Sure am. Can you top her off for me?" Mathis spoke in a terrible British accent to disguise himself.

"Sorry, sir, but we don't have any at the moment. Fueling

truck got overturned on the highway. Need to wait for his replacement."

Mathis' head fell. Rage should've boiled over, but that wasn't the emotion he felt. Only fear.

"We have a restaurant nearby if you'd like to grab something to eat while you wait. Shouldn't be more than an hour or so," the dockhand said.

In his fear, Mathis didn't even comprehend what the young man had said. He simply jumped onto the pier. Once his feet met the concrete, he searched the area for any opposition.

Multiple people were gathered, most smiling and having a great time. Why wouldn't they be? From the outside looking in, those people had it all—the wealthy playing with their toys. Mathis knew that to be true. Without another word to the dockhand, he walked away from the yacht and down the pier.

At the end was a restaurant. His stomach growled at the sight of it. He hadn't eaten in some time. He felt for his pockets. The wad of cash Cleo had given him was still there. When he entered, only a few people were scattered around circular tables. Then a waitress came out holding a tray full of food. The aroma of pancakes, eggs, and bacon filled the air.

"How many?" the hostess asked as she saw him standing there.

Mathis held up one finger.

She grabbed a menu and said, "Follow me."

The hostess led him to the opposite side of the restaurant. He sat with his back to the wall so he could see everyone who entered. She laid the menu down and asked for his drink order.

"Water," he said in the same muddled English accent.

When she walked away, Mathis noticed two TV's hanging above the bar in the corner. A news broadcast was playing. Immediately, Mathis dropped his head, not because he saw himself, but because if he did, he didn't want to be recognized.

When the waitress returned with his water, she asked, "Are you ready to order?"

Mathis nodded. She took out her pad of paper and her pen and waited for him to speak. In her absence, Mathis hadn't even looked at the menu. "Do you have a burger?" this time Mathis forgot the English accent.

"Uh, yes, sir," she looked at him confused.

"I'll have that."

"How would you like it cooked?"

"Medium."

"Anything on it?"

Mathis shook his head, but then said, "Cheese. Cheddar."

"Fries?"

"Sure."

She lifted the menu and moved toward the kitchen, but as she passed the entrance, two policemen entered.

"Hey, Sarah," one of them said.

"Hiya, Aaron. The usual spot?" she said.

They nodded.

"Head over, I'll be there after I put this order in."

They walked directly toward Mathis and sat down at the table next to his.

His heart pumped wildly inside his chest, and he rocked in his seat. They were close enough he could hear their conversation.

"Did you see Marco closed that B&E case up in Diamond Isle?" one cop said to the other.

"I did. Wasn't it pretty much open and shut from the beginning?" the other cop said.

"It was, but the captain was all over his ass for making the arrest."

Mathis raised his head only a little. He didn't mean to, but he caught eyes with the officer who sat across from his partner. Immediately, he ducked away. In doing so, he put too much weight on his right side and sent the water glass tumbling to the ground.

Flustered, he looked up again. This time, both cops stared back at him. In a panic, he jumped from his seat and ran for the door. Both officers rose from their own seats and followed him outside.

Mathis walked down a path that led away from the harbor.

"Sir," one cop shouted from behind.

Mathis didn't pay attention to the call. Instead he scurried away faster.

"Sir. Please stop, we'd like to ask you a few questions."

But he didn't. He set off into a sprint. It was time to flee. He couldn't double back to the harbor, not with nowhere to go. He had to make it on foot. He dodged civilians who congregated around, then sprinted through the parking lot and straight into traffic of Causeway Boulevard.

19

Surrounded by chain-link fencing, I could see the lone wood skiff inside the police impound lot. It was sitting on a flatbed trailer. Not one you would ordinarily see a boat on, but I imagined the sheriff did whatever he had to, to get the abandoned boat out of the water.

From inside Broxton's cruiser, I said, "Did you find anything of use inside the skiff?"

He looked over at me as we waited for the gate to swing open and the guard who manned the lot to move aside.

"No. Nothing."

I sighed.

"What did you expect them to find?" Billy said from the backseat.

"Nothing, I . . . I just want to make sure we're not chasing our tails here."

"So, y'all have a very dangerous fugitive on your hands, don't you?" Broxton asked.

"You're damn right, Sheriff," Billy said.

"What's that like?" His face lit up as he pulled through

the open gate. "You know, like capturing someone on the FBI's top ten list."

I gave him a sideways glance. It was not like he hadn't made arrests in his lifetime as a sheriff. But I imagined—in his small town—he hadn't seen many federal fugitives.

"Mathis isn't your ordinary fugitive."

"No? He like a real bad guy? A throwback to Bonnie and Clyde, you know, that sort of thing?"

"Except there's no pretty girl at the end of a Tommy gun," Billy said.

"No?" I found Billy's eye.

"What?" He paused before filling in the blanks. "You really think that jazz musician is in cahoots with him?"

"Cahoots?" Broxton chuckled. "Ain't heard that word . . . maybe ever."

When the laughter subsided, I answered Billy's question. "I don't, but I'm just sayin' he's had help along the way."

"What do you mean, help?" Billy leaned forward in his seat, just as the sheriff stopped in front of the trailer.

"I mean help. Maybe even somebody on the inside," I said.

There it was. I said it. I didn't want to, but it just hit me.

"Bullshit." Billy couldn't believe it. "That's your theory? He's had help inside the FBI?"

"I don't know about the FBI, but someone has covered his tracks. Why else haven't we been able to track him down all these years?"

"What do you mean?" Broxton asked.

"Yeah, what do you mean?" Billy added.

I stared forward through the windshield, looking at the boat and trying to come up with something. That was the first time that possibility had occurred to me. The more I thought about it though, the more sense it made.

But I didn't have proof, so there was no way I could've answered Billy or the sheriff's question. Instead of speaking, I stepped into the warm air. I instantly started to sweat, and my shirt stuck to my body.

"Uh, what the hell?" Billy joined me and whispered out of earshot of the sheriff.

"What?"

"What do you mean, what? The theory you just dropped on me. How did you come up with it? Where did it come from? You and I have been chasing Mathis together for years—you never once suspected someone from inside the bureau."

"That was then."

"And what? It took you getting shot in the chest by this bastard to have a grand epiphany about one of our own working with him?"

"I didn't say it was someone close. I just said he may have had help, that's all."

I didn't understand why Billy was so defensive. Not until he gave me a line.

"Honor over everything else. Remember the code? It's what we live by in the FBI. Don't embarrass the bureau. You know the crap that Cohen preaches every day. Hell, she blamed you for being too brash. She called you an idiot after you embarrassed yourself and the FBI by getting shot by Mathis in the first place."

I gritted my teeth. Billy's words grew tiresome and were bordering on disrespectful.

"Look. Just forget it, alright. Let's just see what we can

find. Maybe we get lucky and see something the sheriff missed."

Billy threw his hands up in disgust. "I can't believe you." He walked away from the scene just as Broxton came close.

I peered over Broxton's head and watched Billy walk away, incensed. "Trouble in paradise?" he chuckled to himself, then saw I didn't think it was funny and asked, "You really think someone in your own unit was helping this bad guy?"

My mind was spinning, and I still didn't look at Broxton. "Ten minutes ago, no." I continued staring at Billy. "But now . . ." I trailed off and couldn't help but think Billy was involved somehow. *No way a person gets that upset and wasn't involved.* I shifted my attention back to the boat. "Let's just get a couple pictures and get on our way."

But when I took out my phone for the photos, I paused. Thoughts invaded in my mind. Dark thoughts about Billy. No way. He was my friend. He couldn't be crooked. He couldn't break my heart.

After snapping a couple pictures, my phone rang. It was Duda.

"Duda, what is it?"

"Where are you?"

"Police impound near Pensacola, why?"

"Did you hear the latest on your boy?"

"Who? Mathis?"

"Yeah, some chatter came across our line. Apparently, some local cops are in a chase with a man in Clearwater— near the marina and aquarium. A man fitting Mathis' description."

My mouth fell open. "When was this?"

"About five minutes ago."

During the conversation, I followed Billy with my eyes. He was on the phone. Who was he calling? Mathis? No, I was being hasty. While I was still on the line with Duda, Billy called out, "We've got Mathis's location. Just got the call from Cohen. He's in Clearwater."

I heard Billy but didn't respond. To him or Duda.

"James, you there?" Duda said.

"Yeah. Yeah." I fumbled the phone. "I heard you. I've gotta go. Just keep me updated with anything, okay?"

"Got it."

Billy ran back to the car. I met him and he asked. "Who was that?"

"Wrong number." I didn't know why I lied.

"Wrong number?" Billy said.

"That's right."

He studied me. I was a bad liar, and he knew that.

"Interesting," he said, but stopped there.

I was surprised he didn't press further.

"Sheriff Broxton can you take us to the airport?" I said.

"Damn straight. I wanna be a part of this arrest no matter what part I can play. And now I'll have a story to tell my girlfriend. I'll tell her I helped arrest a federal fugitive. That will get her to marry me for sure."

"Marry you?" Billy asked before we stepped in the car. "You proposed?"

We all entered the cruiser.

"Damn straight. Twice."

After I dropped into the front seat, I asked, "And what did she say?"

"Maybe," he said.

"Maybe?" Billy said. "And that's not a red flag to you?"

"Red flag? Hell no, she's just playing hard to get."

"Hard to get?" I couldn't believe it.

"Yeah. You know the type. I mean, she's way out of my league. Used to be a model." He beamed with pride. "But if I help you guys track down a fugitive with this latest intel, she'll come round. She always said she wanted to sleep with a hero. If this doesn't make me a hero, then hell . . . I don't know what will."

After listening to his story, I had to tell him. At least warn him of the heartache he would endure if he did marry that woman.

"Sheriff." He turned the key but waited to shift into drive until I spoke again. "You don't want to marry her," I said.

"I agree," Billy added from the back.

"What do you mean?" he said.

"I mean, she's not worth your time. She sounds like a . . ." I trailed off. I didn't want to offend him.

"Like a what?" he said.

I bit my tongue, but Billy didn't. "A battle-ax, man. Trust me, I've known my share."

"But she's . . . she's so . . . you know," he said.

He didn't have to explain. It was clear that she was out of his league. And it seemed she knew it.

I watched him drop his head. He needed a pick-me-up.

"Tell you what, Sheriff. If—no—when we catch Mathis —we'll let you in on the arrest. You can be there with us when we do it, how'd that be?"

"What?" His face changed from unhappy to elated. "You'd really do that for me?"

"Why not? I figure it would go a long way toward your future career in the FBI wouldn't it, special agent?"

He looked out the window in awe then spoke to himself, "Special Agent. It does have a nice ring to it, doesn't it?"

"Oh, yeah. Now what do you say you flip on those strobes and get us to the airport with haste."

"Oh, don't you worry about that. I drive like a bat out of hell. You two better buckle up. It's about to get real up in this bitch."

20

MATHIS SUCKED IN AIR, STILL TRYING TO CATCH HIS BREATH. He was holed up in a nearby hotel basement. He'd outwitted and outran the police that gave chase, losing them in the traffic that passed over the Causeway Bridge.

He pushed tight against the door of the laundry room that he'd slipped into as a cleaning staff member exited. The room reeked of bleach and detergent as the washing machines tumbled in their spin cycle. The more air Mathis consumed, the woozier his head felt. He needed fresh air soon or he feared he might pass out from the potent fumes. There was a window on the opposite end of the room, but it was high up, near the ceiling.

Mathis walked toward the window and pulled a table close so he could stand on it to reach the latch. The window opened inward. He leaned back to avoid the swinging glass, in doing so, he lost his balance for a moment. The table tilted back on two legs, but before it buckled beneath his feet, Mathis shifted his momentum forward and brought the table upright.

Once the window was open, the familiar squawk of sea gulls echoed in his ears, and the smell of the ocean filled his nostrils instead of the intoxicating chemicals. He smiled, but his relief faded when he heard sirens rebounding around the area.

As he stared out at the ocean, he reached into his pocket and lifted a cell phone. He scrolled to a number with an Atlanta area code and texted.

Help. Police closing in. Need a safe house.

No more than ten seconds passed before he received a response.

Where are you? came the reply.

Clearwater Beach, Mathis wrote back.

Mathis refocused outside. The ocean was close. In the distance there was a fishing vessel offshore. He thought for a moment to cross the road and make the swim to commandeer the boat, but that thought was short lived when he received another prompt answer.

91 Gulf Shores, Clearwater 33755.

It was an address Mathis had never heard of.

Get there and await further instruction.

"Thanks, but how?" Mathis said to himself and stared at the phone.

He looked outside once more, then back at the door. Taking his chances inside the hotel was just as risky as taking his chances outside. If there was some way he could hitch a ride, or maybe steal an unmanned vehicle to reach the address, it would be better than staying put and getting caught.

Mathis reached inside the frame of the window and kicked off the table. His legs were dangling beneath him, and he pulled himself through the small opening. With half of his torso through, he saw the grass below. It was an eight foot drop easy. If he continued out the window, there was a strong chance he would fall face first. But he was committed.

The weight of his body carried him forward. He was nimble enough to curl his head under his shoulders and roll into a summersault. His upper back took the brunt of the jarring force, and his spine cracked as a few vertebrae were shaken loose. But no permanent damage was done.

He rolled out of the summersault and into a sprint toward the ocean. There was a parking lot nearby. It was half full of cars. He stared inside each of the windows looking for keys and tried every driver side door. Nothing. Not one was unlocked.

Sirens grew closer and closer until three squad cars came racing down Mandalay Avenue from the north. Mathis ducked behind a car. His heart pounded in his chest and from his crouched position, he watched as the squad cars rounded the corner and drove directly into the hotel parking lot.

As he watched them turn, he saw a pink scooter with matching helmet secured on the back seat with mesh cloth. He ran toward it and mounted the side, then rocked forward to get the scooter off its kickstand. He secured the helmet—it was a little small, but felt he needed to disguise himself. He couldn't believe his luck: the key was still in the ignition. He moved the kill switch to the run position and kickstarted it.

On the first kick, the engine revved to life. He spun the throttle and drove toward Mandalay Avenue. More police sped south, and he waited for them to pass before pulling into the northbound lane.

. . .

LETTING OFF THE THROTTLE, Mathis lowered his speed, being careful not to miss 91 Gulf Shores. The street was a quiet cul-de-sac. Every house looked the same—the builder stuck with what worked. The only way he could tell the difference between each home was by the address and color.

91 Gulf shores was colored salmon pink. Maybe coral in the state of Florida. Either way, it was hideous.

Mathis steered into the driveway and killed the engine, then rocked back on the kickstand to stand the moped upright. After unbuckling the helmet, he walked toward the house. At the front door, he peered through the small windows on both sides of the front door, but they were tinted and he couldn't see what was inside.

He reached for the doorbell, but quickly pulled his hand back. He didn't want to alert anyone around the area with the sound, just in case the bell was loud, or the walls were thin. Instead he grabbed the handle. To his surprise, the door was unlocked. He pushed inside and gently closed the door behind him. He was about to say hello, but again he knew silence was best.

The house was mostly empty aside from one couch in the living area with a small TV. Not a nice TV—an old tube television. He continued into the kitchen. Again, it was barren. He opened the cabinets. There were a few pots and pans and a couple plates. In the cabinet by the fridge there were a ton of cans of non-perishable food.

After the kitchen, he walked through the hallway and toward the only bedroom. The door was closed. He thought to knock but realized that was dumb. No one was there. It was completely empty. But when he opened the door, his eyes met a grisly scene.

Blood was spattered everywhere. The walls. The ceiling. And there was a stained pool on the floor. Even the pale white bed sheets were blood red.

Mathis yanked the door shut.

"What the hell?"

He grabbed the phone from his pocket and texted his contact: *Is the body still here?*

The imaginary smell of dried blood swam into his nostrils—a smell his mind conjured up just thinking about the possibility of a dead man in the house.

No body. Just the aftermath.

Mathis wanted to know more.

Who's the body?

Someone who got too close. Just stay put, you're safe there.

"Stay put? I can't stay here, what if the cops followed the stolen scooter?" Mathis said to himself.

He was already in a world of pain after shooting an FBI agent. His mind raced. "I can't stay . . . not in the middle of . . . of some murder scene."

21

As we sped through traffic, I glanced back at Billy. He was looking at his phone, intently reading a text. He witnessed me staring, then gave me a subtle smile and slipped his phone back into his pocket.

"What?" I said needing to know who he was talking to.

Without skipping a beat, he said, "Boss set up a plane for us to fly to the St. Pete-Clearwater airport."

"Really?" I said, wondering why she hadn't included me on the text.

"Yeah. Also asked why we got split up with Deputy Kill. Said he was pretty pissed off that we left him behind. Apparently, he's gonna meet us on the plane."

"Pssh, that was my doing," Broxton said. "I didn't want that condescending bastard in my car."

Billy chuckled, but I didn't. I was more focused on how Billy had done it? How could he do it? Helping Mathis all these years? Did he tell Mathis where I'd be? The devil spun my thoughts like a top, playing me perfectly. Knowing precisely the right strings to pull. Instead of Mathis, it was basically like Billy had pulled the trigger and shot me himself.

I found his eye again. He could tell something was eating at me.

"What?" he said.

After all we'd been through, he knew me better than my own wife—or ex-wife—it would seem.

"Nothing." I turned back around.

"What's your problem?"

I sighed. I wanted to have it out with him. Get it out in the open. But my back was to him, and if he was the evil mastermind I thought he was, he'd have the advantage of pulling his piece and aiming it at my back.

"I said, *nothing*."

Broxton eyed me from the driver's seat. "Uh, oh. You two having a lover's quarrel?"

"Hell no," I said.

"Bullshit," Billy added. "I know you. You're acting like you've got something on me—like I betrayed your trust or something."

Did he know? Of course, he did. He was the one conspiring with Mathis behind my back.

"It's nothing." I still wasn't going to let on what was bothering me. Not until I was certain about the betrayal.

"Then stop acting like a punk," Billy said.

Then Broxton added insult to injury. "You are kinda being a little baby."

I glared at him. "Looks like you don't want that recommendation into the FBI after all, do you, sheriff?"

"I . . . uh . . . um," Broxton mumbled and backtracked.

"Alright, alright, take it easy," Billy said.

The rest of the way we drove in silence. But it didn't take

more than five minutes for us to arrive at the airstrip. Of course Kill was already there. His arms were folded, and his face was stern.

Broxton stopped in front of the plane, and we all stepped out. Broxton opened his mouth to speak, but Kill cut him off. "I don't need any lip from you, Barney Fife. This is between me and the two boys here."

Broxton lowered his brow and seethed but didn't respond to Kill. Instead, he moved to the driver's side door. But before he dropped in, he said, "Don't forget about me when you make the arrest."

"Never," I said.

Once Broxton drove away, Kill added more fuel to the fire. "Where did Sheriff Marshmallow bring you?"

"Easy, Kill. He's a good man," I said.

"That may be true, but that still doesn't explain why you left me on the docks with the witness and took off with the sheriff on your own."

"We went to look at the boat," Billy said. "The one the big guy lent Mathis. It was in police impound."

"And? What did you find?" Kill said.

"Nothing," I said.

"Nothing." Kill laughed. "Figures."

"But Duda did tell me about Mathis," I said. "He's in Clearwater."

"What are we waiting for then?" Kill said.

"Those buffalo skin boots to work their way into the plane." Billy nodded at Kill's feet.

Honestly, I hadn't taken notice that he changed them. They weren't the same ones he had on in the field office in Jacksonville. These were nicer. Something you'd wear to impress. Not on a stakeout or manhunt.

"Better to stomp the life out of a man." Kill raised his foot.

"Whatever gets the job done," Billy said, then walked up the staircase that was attached to the plane.

"Where's your partner?" I said.

"Had to get back to the office."

Really? Honestly, I figured he'd be joining us the rest of the hunt, but, guess not.

I tried to follow Billy up the stairs, but Kill cut off my path. He stared right through me. The man could level you with his eyes—and not in a good way. He reached out his bear claw that he called a hand and wrapped his fingers around my neck, then squeezed.

"Don't you dare pull one over on me again. Understand, kid?"

His grip was so tight that I could feel my blood getting trapped beneath his fingertips. I nodded up and down before there was too much blood loss to my brain.

"Because if you do." He paused and sucked in a breath. "I'll cut your dick off while you sleep." He winked, then let go and followed Billy inside.

I was powerless. Never felt so . . . so weak. Not from any man. Nor any suspect I'd ever encountered. Kill held a dominance over me. Something unforeseen. He knew it and I knew it. I would never piss that man off again.

22

Mathis's mind spun as he paced the kitchen. His stomach growled more than once when he caught sight of the canned food that stared back at him through the open cabinet doors. But how could he eat at a time like that? With the murder scene still lingering in his mind? Mathis had been a thief his entire life, but truth be told, he had never been able to stomach the sight of blood. Especially that much blood.

His mind continued to swirl as he imagined what had happened to the poor soul who was on the receiving end of the gruesome demise.

"Damnit, no." He shook his head from side to side. "Don't go there."

He forced the evil away, then moved to the cupboard. A can of spaghetti and meatballs stared back at him. Bile rose in his gut, and he gagged. The red-orange liquid and the twisting noodles reminded him too much of brains. The brains that may have been left behind on the floor of the room.

He slammed the door shut and grabbed his mouth, forcing the acid back down into his stomach. He couldn't take staying there. Both from the anxiety his weak mind created and because he didn't want to be caught with his hand in the cookie jar.

Mathis moved toward the front door and peered outward. The street was quiet. Not so much as a passing car drove by, but why would there be? There were only three houses in the cul-de-sac. If there was a lot of traffic, that would've stirred up suspicion.

The pink scooter was right where he left it. He walked outside and mounted the seat. He spun the key and tried to kickstart it. After multiple failed attempts, Mathis perspired and breathed heavy. No matter what he tried, the engine wouldn't turn over. The fuel gauge still read a quarter tank.

"Come on, you bastard." He tried again. And again. But still, nothing.

Mathis dumped the scooter in the yard and ran back inside.

He moved through the hallway and toward the back of the home. There was a door there. As he walked, he passed the shut bedroom door the nightmarish scene was locked behind. He refused to even look at the door. He just kept his eyes forward. When he reached the back door, he stared into the yard.

A stockpile of weeds grew almost two feet high. The front yard was perfectly manicured, but this . . . no one kept up with the sprouting foliage.

The property was lined with a chain-link fence that backed to a park. The park looked just as rundown as the back yard. The weeds weren't growing as high, but the playground equipment was battered down by rust and time. One swing was broken at the chain, and the other was wrapped around the top of the frame almost all the way to the top.

Mathis opened the door and stepped outside. He breathed the air. It smelled fresh. Maybe fresher than any he'd smelled in a long time. He looked toward the sun and closed his eyes to feel the warmth on his face. Why he did it, he didn't know.

When he opened his eyes again, he knew it was time to go. But before Mathis could take a step, his phone buzzed— or at least he thought it did. He lifted the phone from his pocket. There were no new messages. Only then could he think of the last thing his contact had told him:

Stay put. You're safe there.

Safe? For whom? Mathis hadn't felt safe inside the house ever since he witnessed the bloody scene.

He didn't wait. He couldn't wait. He walked through the gate and into the park. There was a street in front of the park, and Mathis walked toward it. Just as he did, a police cruiser sped by. Mathis stopped walking and instinctively dropped his head.

The cruiser wasn't in a hurry, at least not then. No lights. No sirens.

Once the car was out of sight, Mathis continued toward the road. It was a busy street. A lot more traffic drove by. He looked to his right, then left. He was a bit turned around and didn't know which way was which. He looked toward the sun and did his best to calculate his orientation.

The best he could come up with was that right was northeast and left was southwest. Southwest would've led him closer to the hotel, so he chose the opposite direction. With no idea where it would lead, Mathis remained on the sidewalk.

There were bricks laid in a herringbone pattern—the same design on the connecting driveway. Their garage was open too, but no one was around. A car sat in the garage with the engine on. Mathis paused a moment, then took one step into the driveway and toward the running car. The car was empty. The homeowner must've run back inside to get something.

Excitement grew in his belly. This could be it. His way out.

He crept forward, being careful not to make a sound. When he was about to enter the garage, someone—a woman—from inside the house opened the door. He ducked out of sight and crouched behind the trunk.

The woman was paying attention to her cell phone and didn't see Mathis. She opened the driver's side door and fell inside.

Mathis rubbed the back bumper. He wanted the car— no, needed the car. But for some reason he resisted the urge to throw her out and steal it.

Even he didn't know why. For some reason, he decided to spare her the grief of being carjacked. When he heard the car shift into reverse, Mathis scurried away from the bumper and toward the side of the house. Still paying attention to her cell phone, the woman didn't see him move.

From the side of the house, Mathis watched her pull away onto the street and disappear. As he stared, he wondered if he'd done the right thing. The car was there. So easy to take. But the panicked call from another victim would've brought the police closer to his position.

If he was going to steal a getaway vehicle, it had to be in secret.

23

DURING THE FLIGHT, I WAS CONSUMED WITH THOUGHTS OF betrayal. I couldn't help but think that if we got close, Billy would turn on me. But how would he evade the watchful eye of Kill too?

More intel came in from Cohen while we were on the plane. The search of the hotel in Clearwater came up empty, and a report of a stolen pink scooter adjacent to the hotel property was also filed.

They had to be connected. I wondered how far Mathis could really get on a scooter. Maybe fifty miles on a full tank of gas.

When the plane stopped rolling, I unlatched my seatbelt and walked to the front of the plane. I had to be the first one off.

There was a car waiting for us on the tarmac, but no driver. I paused, but Kill didn't. He breezed by and said, "I'm driving, y'all."

Fine by me. I didn't know Clearwater well. Not that finding the hotel and the beach would be hard, but driving in my enraged state probably wasn't the best thing for any of us. Although, I would've preferred the distraction.

When I moved to the back of the black sedan, the trunk was open. Out of curiosity, I looked inside. Three thick duffel bags lay there. I unzipped one. The contents included a bulletproof vest, an M4 carbine semi-automatic assault rifle with three extra mags, and an additional Glock 23 with extra mags as well.

We were well stocked to take down Mathis—or a small army. I imagined the two other duffels housed similar contents.

"Thanks to the US Marshals," Kill said. "We'll just charge it to the FBI."

Kill slammed the trunk shut, then proceeded to the front seat. I followed suit and dropped into the car.

Kill started the engine, and I couldn't help but ask, "You know where you're going?"

"Straight into the lion's den, kid," Kill said.

I looked over at him. "Wait, what?"

Kill's eyes were thin. He knew something he wasn't letting on.

"You know where he is, don't you?" I couldn't help but ask the question I knew hung in his eyes.

"I have an inkling."

"How?" Billy spoke from the backseat.

"I had a friend hack into the department of transportation. They got an eye on the pink scooter and followed it to one specific area."

"Serious?" I couldn't mask my excitement.

"As a dead man, kid."

Kill drove on, then Billy spoke again. "Don't you think we should start at the hotel? Gather more intel first?"

I whipped my head around. *What? No, you idiot.* No agent in their right mind would start at the source. Not if we had the element of surprise on our hands. His question just confirmed my suspicion.

"Why would we do that?" I said. Could he really have a substantiated argument?

"What if the scooter wasn't Mathis? What if the theft was a coincidence, or he paid someone to throw us off the trail?

I stopped. Honestly, his theory held water.

"Knowing Mathis, he's more apt to steal a boat than a scooter," Billy added.

You'd know him best. But I wasn't about to say that.

I glanced over at Kill. I wanted to know what his thoughts were.

"Tell you what. If you want to chase down the hotel lead, be my guest, but I'm checking into the scooter."

I looked back at Billy. I was sure he was thinking I would side with him. Why wouldn't I? After all we'd been through. We were friends. Had done more than a few cases together. Together 'til the end. But I didn't trust his judgement, not then.

"I agree with Kill."

Billy's mouth fell open.

"Let's check out the scooter first," I said.

There was disappointment in Billy's eyes.

KILL STOPPED AT AN INTERSECTION, then pulled off to the side of the road and shifted into park.

As he looked up at the stop light above, I asked. "Is that where your source saw him?"

I looked out my window and down the street. It was your typical everyday quiet suburb street. The sign above read: *Gulf Shores*.

"This is where the camera saw him turn right." Kill pointed. "And drive down Gulf Shores."

"This is ridiculous," Billy rocked in the back seat. "Mathis didn't go down some quiet suburb street on a pink scooter. He probably hid out in the hotel. Hunkered down until the police left the area. Then he'll double back to the marina and boost another boat."

I couldn't believe him. What was he saying? He didn't want us to close in on Mathis. He was afraid Mathis would give him up.

"What makes you say that?" Kill said, looking at him through the rearview mirror.

Billy stalled and remained quiet. Quiet enough to hear the buzz of someone's cell phone vibrate in their pocket. I eyed Billy. Sweat started to bead on his forehead.

"My gut tells me this is foolish. And we know Mathis." Billy nodded at me. "This goes against everything we know about him."

He was right. Mathis did usually flee the country. He didn't stick around long enough to get caught. Not in some suburb of Clearwater, Florida.

"We've already established he's gone outside the norm of his behavior by shooting your friend. So . . . you're telling me you're willing to let the man walk who shot James in the chest?" Kill asked.

Billy's next words would tell me everything I needed to know.

He huffed. Then nodded and said, "Go on then. Prove me wrong."

Kill turned down Gulf Shores. He drove slowly. I was on the edge of my seat, scanning the area for any sign of the pink scooter.

Every house looked the same—aside from some whose lawns were in pristine order.

An elderly woman worked on her hands and knees, digging through her bed of mulch. She leaned back to stretch when she caught sight of our car. Kill offered a wave, but she didn't so much as smile.

You could tell she didn't recognize the car—and she wore a look that said we were unwelcome in her neighborhood.

"This is it. I can feel it," Kill said.

How could he be so sure?

Three more houses passed by, and then I saw a cul-de-sac upcoming. As we came upon it, Kill pushed the brakes down hard and jolted me forward.

There. In the front yard—laying on the grass at 91 Gulf Shores—was a pink scooter and matching helmet.

I spun around and caught Billy's eye.

"That doesn't prove anything," he said. "Only that some twenty something—messy college student lives here."

"Or the man who shot me twice in the chest," I said.

Billy nodded and rolled his eyes, then reached for the handle like he was looking to prove me wrong.

I looked over at Kill and said, "Should we call for backup?"

"Hell no, kid. I *am* your backup."

Excitement grew in my belly. I knew we had him. I knew we had Mathis.

But before we could even exit, Billy spoke up, "Leave the keys in the ignition."

"What was that?" I said.

"You heard me. I'm going to the hotel. If you two want to follow up on this lead, go ahead, but I'm not sticking around for it."

"What? We're working this case together." How could he abandon me now? There was only one possible scenario.

"It seems you'd rather listen to Kill anyhow. You heard him. He's your backup."

"So, what . . . you're just gonna leave?" I said.

"That's right. I'm going with my gut here too, ya know."

I was speechless. Kill was already halfway out the door when he said, "If he wants to go, let him. We got this. Just pop the trunk so we can grab our gear."

I stepped out of the car, and Billy walked to the driver's seat. Before dipping in, he said, "Be careful."

So what? Now, you're concerned with my safety? If you really were, you'd stay and back me up. But I couldn't tell him that. His mind was made.

Kill lifted two bags, slinging one across my shoulder, before slamming the trunk shut.

Billy said only one other thing. And that stayed with me. "You're just going to have to trust me."

Trust him? How could I? He was leaving me in the greatest time of need. But as I watched him pull away, there was some trace—some part of me, no matter how small— that still did.

24

THERE WAS A CURVE COMING UP IN THE ROADWAY. MATHIS saw the outline of a bridge. He couldn't tell what kind, not yet. Was it built over water? Maybe another roadway? At the sight of it, a fire was lit inside him, and he went from a swift walk into a jog.

Palm trees lined both sides of the road, and near the bridge there were thicker shrubs. As Mathis ran further, he saw an opening in the bushes. And through that opening, there was blue water.

Once he caught sight of the water, he no longer bothered with the sidewalk path. Neglecting to look over his shoulder, he stepped into the road and jogged to the median. He stopped and waited for no less than eight cars to pass by before he could continue.

"Come on. Come on."

He waved them on while staring at the freedom that the water promised. It looked so inviting. He had no idea if it was a small pond or a waterway that connected to the intercoastal, but in that moment it didn't matter—he was hell-bent on reaching it.

When the final car passed, Mathis sprinted across the street and onto someone's property. He didn't care about trespassing. Besides, from the look of the tattered white house, it had to be vacant.

Mathis walked through the gap of trees and reached the water. Looking out, he saw the river flowing and the current pulling westward. There was a ripple in the water, like a boat with a small motor had recently passed by.

That was his way out. His way back to the intercoastal and eventually back to the ocean.

Mathis glanced behind him, then searched the area for something to use as a floatation device. Swimming freely was his last resort. There was no sign of an alligator nearby, but that didn't mean one wasn't lurking below the surface or sunbathing along the opposite shore ready to dip in the water and swim close out of curiosity.

A downed tree—split in half—laid in the brush beside him. Not ideal, but it was something he could feed into the current and drift on while staying above the water line. He continued searching, but there was nothing but shrubbery.

Mathis bit down hard on his lip. He didn't have time to wait around. What if some random patrol car drove by and happened to see him? Or the homeowner came outside and approached with a weapon? Mathis needed to act.

He grabbed the end of the log and pulled it free from the bush that held it tight. Once the log was set into the water, Mathis walked deeper, pulling the log along with him.

His body went tense at the temperature. He didn't

remember the water being that cold near Orange Beach. Perhaps it was the adrenaline of jumping onto a yacht that had kept him warm. Now though, the water felt frigid on his skin.

When the water level rose to his waist, the current began to pull him. Mathis reached for the floating log, and once he caught hold of it, the log dipped below the surface and sank.

Mathis wasn't expecting the log to sink under his weight, but it did. Once he let go, the log resurfaced. He grabbed hold again to support his weight, but again, the log sank.

Mathis stood tall and slapped the water with his open palm. "Damnit."

The log was useless.

Mathis watched the log drift away on its own as he stood in the water. He needed to trudge along and stay at that depth until he could find a skiff, canoe, kayak, anything. The thought of leaving the water and backtracking to the marina via the street entered his mind. It would've been a bold attempt. Maybe he could get there without being seen, refuel the stolen yacht, and set sail for Key West—if he could make it that far.

But that wasn't realistic.

Mathis stepped through the water, but his foot got stuck in the mucky bottom. As he ripped his leg free from the mud, a flash of green caught his eye. He paused, focused on the shoreline, and saw a canoe.

Mathis lumbered toward the edge of the water and saw the canoe pushed into a thicket of trees. It was out of place —or maybe it wasn't. Through the dense tree line was another house, built beneath overhanging oaks and cedars.

No one was around, at least not outside. The carport was also empty.

He rolled the canoe over and placed it in the water. It floated. Then he searched the shore for a paddle. Nothing. Not in the direct vicinity. But after looking at the home again, he saw a twenty-three-foot Ranger Bass Boat trailered near the exterior of the home.

Against the trailer was a stack of paddles. Mathis looked to the water again. He wouldn't get very far without a paddle. Although he was in a canoe, he'd still be at the mercy of the tide and current.

He pulled the canoe back ashore and stepped through the thick foliage. He stopped to gather his wits and bearings, making sure any adjoining properties were also vacant.

He snuck across the backyard and toward the stack of paddles pushed against the trailer parked under the second story deck. When he reached the starboard side, he reached down and grabbed the first one he saw. It was small and flimsy. One you'd use for a children's blowup raft.

He set it back down, but it fell harder than he wanted it to, and it slid off the stack of others and clattered into a pile of wood that laid nearby. He paused, making sure nobody had heard his mistake. No one did. He picked up another. This one was nicer—a two-piece aluminum paddle. Super lightweight and easy to propel through the water.

"Jackpot," he said, then turned around.

But just as he turned, a man pumped his Remington twelve-gauge and pointed it directly at his chest.

"Put the paddle down," the man said.

Shocked, Mathis gulped and did as he was told.

"You trying to steal my canoe?" the man nodded beyond Mathis and toward the river.

Mathis gritted his teeth and held his tongue.

"You that man on television? The one they say shot the federal agent?"

Mathis was caught. "I . . . I . . ."

"The police are already on their way."

Just as he spoke, Mathis heard the sirens in the distance.

"Please, sir," Mathis begged.

"Maybe I just shot you dead here. You are on my property—trespassing—I'm well within my rights to watch you die." The man nodded to the ground. "Here at my feet."

Mathis was stuck. But he couldn't wait around. Not for the police. And not for the man to get an itchy trigger finger and blast a shot of buckshot through his sternum.

Mathis blinked slow, then cut tail and ran. The man was taken by surprise, because it was about a two second delay before Mathis heard the first blast of buckshot explode in his ear as he sprinted toward the canoe.

25

Bang. Bang.

Shots rang out in the distance, and they stopped me in my tracks, even before I could approach the front door of the house.

"Did you hear that?" I asked Kill.

The question was rhetorical. Of course he did.

Kill nodded and tuned his ear toward the sound. He was waiting for more. One more shot came. Then another.

Kill whipped his head around. "Damnit," he said. "We should've never let Lyons go."

"You think that was Mathis?" I said.

"Had to be."

I ran into the road and tried to see Billy, but the sedan was parked at the light and waiting to turn left.

"Billy," I yelled and waved my arms. "Stop. Billy."

But he didn't. Either he didn't see me or didn't care. I reached down and grabbed my phone and called him. Straight to voicemail. "Shit." I forced my hand down. Then dialed him again. Straight to voicemail. "Shit."

I looked around for Kill, but he was nowhere to be found.

"Deputy Kill?" I stared around the side of the house and caught sight of him hopping the fence in the backyard.

I jammed the phone back into my pocket and chased him down.

He ran through an old park. He was ahead of me, and I wasn't gaining much ground. "Damn he's fast," I muttered to myself.

My lungs burned, and I got a stitch in my side. The bag was heavy too—had to be upwards of twenty-five pounds worth of gear. But I had to push through the ache. Holy hell, I was out of shape. How could a man almost twice my age keep the pace he did? He was an ironman.

Sirens echoed in the distance when I made it to the park. Kill must've heard them too, because we followed the sound. They were closing in and speeding fast.

When I caught him, I said, "Go to the sirens." As if he didn't know. Two squad cars rushed at our position. Then they whipped a right turn about 200 yards before us, turning down a shaded street. One you'd ordinarily pass by on any given day because you didn't know it was there.

WE FOLLOWED the path of the squad cars. When we caught sight of them, their sirens were turned off, but there was still flashing blue and red beneath the darkened trees.

When we got close, I heard a man's voice. It was deep and throaty. He was upset and yelling. But it seemed his anger was directed at someone who had been on his property and stolen his canoe rather than the police.

When we made it to the property, I saw two police taking the man's statement and two more checking the perimeter for any sign of the intruder.

The policeman saw us and were about to usher us away when we pulled our badges. They nodded but eyed us funny. We must have looked weird. Both of us were still carrying our duffel bags.

"What do we have?" Kill asked the officer who pulled away from the witness.

"A man came onto Mr. Winston's property and stole a paddle and a canoe."

I eyed Mr. Winston. His hat was cocked to the side of his head, and there were enough oil stains on his tattered flannel shirt to catch fire if he touched a flame.

"Mr. Winston." I stepped toward him. "My name is Special Agent Jasper James with the FBI." Again, I flashed my badge.

Before Mr. Winston could respond, an officer did. "What's this about?"

"I'm sure you're aware of the situation, but we're after a federal fugitive." I directed my attention to the officer who asked the question.

"Sure. I heard something over the radio," the officer said.

"We have reason to believe that the man who stole your canoe is that very same man." I looked back to Mr. Winston.

"You sure about that, chief?" the officer said. "I heard your man was trapped in a hotel down in Clearwater Beach."

"And what . . . you just happen to think this was a coincidence this man's canoe was stolen?"

I couldn't believe the officer could be that shortsighted.

He gave me a sideways glance.

"Let me prove it to you," I said. "Mr. Winston, how often would you say you have theft around here?"

"Oh, uh, not often?"

"Ever?" I urged him forward.

"No, I guess not. I've never had to defend my property with lethal force if that's what you mean. At least not until today."

"That's exactly what I mean. So, like I said, this man you saw, could you describe him for me?"

"Oh, uh, sure. I guess, he was about this high." Mr. Winston put his hand above his head. "Medium build. Maybe in his mid to late forties. White. Dark hair."

I'd asked him to describe the thief before I led with the picture because I didn't want to sway his decision before he was able to offer me his own explanation.

"Was this the man you saw?" I lifted Mathis' picture.

"Yeah, that's that little sonofabitch right there." He shook his head and pointed at the picture.

I thanked him, then looked beyond him and onto his property.

"Can you show me where he shoved the canoe into the water?"

"Yes, sir. Follow me." He waved us forward.

As we walked, I took note of the man's property. It was heavily wooded—very private. It was the sort of place I would've tried to take something from. I'm sure Mathis thought the same thing. He just got unlucky.

"It's right up here." Mr. Winston kept walking. "There." He pointed through a small opening in the trees that led directly to the water.

"Thank you, sir." I nodded, then walked to the shoreline and looked out.

The river was narrow—only about 150 yards across.

Kill caught up and looked over me.

I turned around and yelled back to Mr. Winston, "Where does this water lead?"

"Into Clearwater Bay," he said.

"Could one paddle back to the marina?"

"Yeah, sure. I might take you while—an hour or so—but you could definitely get there."

I stared at Kill.

"Maybe Lyons was on to something?" Kill said.

"Yeah, maybe," I said.

Or maybe that was their plan all along. I didn't want to say it, not to Kill. I didn't want to put Billy in his crosshairs too, just in case I was wrong. Problem was though, everything that had happened over the past few hours led me to believe that wasn't the case.

"You know much about canoes?" I asked Kill.

"No. Why?"

"Hey, Mr. Winston?"

"Yes, sir."

"How long would it take the average person to paddle from here into the bay?"

"Depends on the wind and tide."

"How about right now?" I looked to the water.

Mr. Winston came closer to have a look at the water. Kill stepped out of his way and allowed him space. "Based on the wind, tide, and current, I'd say about twenty to thirty minutes, max."

"And how long ago did he leave here?" I pointed to the shore.

"Five—ten minutes."

"Thank you, sir. Let's go talk to the officers," I told Kill.

I walked back onto the property and said, "Excuse me?" I wanted to see who spoke up, because he was the man in charge in that situation.

"How can I help you, Agent James?" the officer said, the one I originally met with upon our arrival.

"Do you know where this waterway leads?"

"Yes, sir. There's a bridge out on North Fort."

"Can you get some men posted there?"

"When?"

"Now."

The officer stalled, then said, "I have more men coming here now. Should I reroute them?"

"Yes. Tell them to shut down the road in both directions and be on the lookout for a man in a canoe."

The officer nodded and leaned toward his shoulder to relay the new information into his radio.

"How about a chopper?" I said.

"I know we had one circling down by the hotel," he said.

"Call it up here. To that bridge."

"I don't know that I have that kind of pull, but I'll try," he said.

"And Officer," I said.

"Yes, sir."

"How far away are we from that bridge?"

"No more than five minutes."

"Can we use one of your squad cars?" I asked.

"Sure. Keys are in it. Just head west on Fairmont to North Fort Harrison Avenue. Turn right and the bridge won't be more than a half mile away."

"Thank you."

He nodded, then I looked to Kill, who was already standing by my side. "You coming?" I said.

"Damn right," he said.

We opened the back door to the vehicle and both threw in our duffel bags. Then I got into the driver's side and sped away.

26

BLOOD SOAKED THROUGH MATHIS' PANTS, AND HE COULD FEEL the liquid beneath his butt as he sat on the stool. Two pellets of buckshot were lodged into the back of his leg. It was near impossible for him to see where the shots had entered. He removed his shirt and tied a tourniquet as high up on his thigh as he could, but still he didn't know if it would be enough.

His heart pumped as he paddled with his arms. Being shot changed things. Shelter was his only option. He needed to get inside—find another house. Somewhere he could play surgeon. But again, with the location of the shots, surgery would be a chore.

On the opposite side of the riverbank, there was an inlet. He couldn't know where it led, but there were enough trees and shrubs in the way to act as cover.

He paddled toward the inlet, and once he got close, he grabbed for the overhanging branches to pull them out of his way.

The water was shallow and had the appearance of a

drainage ditch. It was no more than two feet deep, but still deep enough for a canoe to fit. As he splashed through the narrow opening, he could see that the waterway led toward a bridge and another roadway.

More sirens blared out and echoed. He couldn't be sure of their location because of how disorienting the sound became, but they were close and so was the bridge. Mathis cupped his hands and tore through the water as fast as he could. Once he came to the bridge, he realized it was going to be a tight squeeze for the canoe to fit under—tighter than it looked from farther off. Less than three feet of clearance separated the bow of the canoe and the concrete from the bottom of the bridge.

Mathis leaned back and fell flat—lying parallel. Just as he disappeared beneath the bridge, two squad cars raced over the road just above him. The vibration rumbled the boat and shook him.

Mathis waited for only another moment before reaching up to the bottom of the bridge. He used the underside as a handhold and pulled himself along. Light filtered through the opposite end. From his position, he couldn't tell if the river was the same on the other side. Maybe it opened up more—somehow became wider—or maybe the trees and shrubs would close in on him further.

When the bow breached the opening, more of the river revealed itself. Overgrown trees and brush canopied the water.

It was a good thing too, because just as Mathis pushed under the bridge completely, he heard the rumblings of a helicopter thundering from overhead.

There were two homes to his right and three more to his

left. Each was backed to the river and had a chain-link fence separating the land from the public water of the river.

The homes were old. Some in better condition than others. One owner didn't take care of their backyard—that much was easy to see from the unkempt tall grass, much like the 91 Gulf Shores house.

Mathis steered toward the shoreline, then raised up and hobbled on one leg, before pulling himself out of the boat. He spied the area—the entire area, looking at all the houses within his field of vision. Not one person lingered outside. But one of the homes on the north side of the water had its light on. He could see through the window. A man—probably in his seventies—was moving about in his kitchen.

Mathis was careful not to make any noise as he reached for a gate on the south side of the water. The latch was rusty and squeaked as he raised it. He paused, but once the gate was open, he hobbled away from the shore and into the yard.

On the grass, he limped, but he limped with purpose. He counted on no one being home, because if someone was and they saw him, they'd call the police, and he would have nowhere else to run. But really, how much farther could he even go?

At that point, he was tired of running. His urge to survive had faded. Sure, he was afraid of getting caught and more jail time . . . deep down though, he was questioning everything. Including his own salvation. Death was coming for him, like an old friend. But he wasn't ready, not then.

On the back of the house, there was a white screen door covered with at least four layers of chipped paint. Mathis couldn't bother with checking the windows before he entered, not then. His only option was to hope—no, pray—that the back door was open and no one was home.

Mathis held his breath. The screen clicked open, and he grabbed for the handle. It spun. He let go of that breath and pushed the door open—forgetting about the potential of an alarm, or worse, a barking dog.

Neither warning came.

"Hel-lo?" Mathis said.

There was no answer.

He stepped inside and said hello again. But again, no answer.

The back door led him into the kitchen. Dishes were strewn about—tossed everywhere—which indicated someone had left in a rush, or they were messy.

Inside the dining room attached to the kitchen, there was a collection of yarn and thread. And a sewing magazine rested on the table near a sewing machine.

"At least she's got needles if it comes to that," Mathis mumbled to himself.

Everything inside the house pointed to a woman home-owner. Mathis didn't bother to check the rest of the property. He needed to find a first aid kit.

To his left, Mathis saw a door. It was cracked open, and the flooring was tiled. Mathis walked toward it and just as he was about to enter, something skirted across the floor. Mathis jumped back in fright at the tiny feline who ran down the hallway.

"Damned cat." He put his hand to his chest.

With the next step he took, he could feel fresh blood start to drip down his hamstring before slithering down the back of his knee.

The white tile on the bathroom floor was muted in color

by dirt and grime. There was no way it had been cleaned in months, maybe years. Mathis was starting to get the feeling this wouldn't be the most sterile environment to fix his wounds.

A mirrored medicine cabinet hung on the wall above the sink. Mathis opened it, and quickly saw a few orange prescriptions bottles. He hoped for Codeine or Oxycodone, something to numb the pain. But it was not to be. After reading the labels, Mathis realized the medicine was for an Alzheimer's patient.

He set the bottles down and searched for anything else he could use. After gathering as many supplies as he could find, Mathis moved out of the bathroom and into the bedroom.

The bedroom was the cleanest room in the house. And as he moved inside, he found something: a full-length mirror pushed against the wall.

Mathis limped near and dropped his pants. They stuck at first, which caused him to wince, but after pulling hard, he was able to get them to his ankles. All he could see was charred red and black. There was no skin, not even a piece of leg hair was visible beneath the blood.

With no exit wounds through the thigh, clearly both pellets remained lodged in his muscle.

Things looked bleak. There was no way he could operate on himself. Too much risk for infection. Too much risk for blood loss.

There was only one thing left to do: text his contact and ask for help.

He lifted the phone from his pocket and texted.

911. Been shot. If I can't get help soon, I'll be dead by morning.

A text came back. *Where are you?*

Mathis didn't know the address. He hobbled back through the kitchen and found a stack of unopened mail and typed in the number and street.

Help is on the way.

27

WHEN WE REACHED THE BRIDGE, THE COPS HAD JUST ARRIVED. There was a man in uniform stopping traffic on both ends, and other officers inside their squad cars were parking perpendicular to the bridge to block off any incoming traffic.

We were three cars back from the first civilian vehicle that had attempted to turn around. The road wasn't wide, and there was hardly any shoulder, so turning around would take time . . . time we didn't have.

"Screw this," Kill said as he dropped his phone into his pocket before stepping out. "Map says there isn't much around here."

I shoved the car into park and flicked on the strobes before getting out and walking toward the bridge.

Kill was jogging ahead when I saw a policeman stop him. "This road is closed, sir, please get back into your vehicle."

The cop had no idea we just got out of a squad car. Kill lifted his badge and the policeman allowed him through.

I was right behind Kill when I flashed my badge too.

"FBI and the Marshal Service? This guy is high priority," the cop said as we ran by.

Kill moved to the center of the bridge, lifted his sidearm, and stared at the open water. I did the same, then looked to my watch.

Kill saw me and asked, "How much time has passed since he escaped in the canoe?"

"By Mr. Winston's calculations? I'd say close to fifteen minutes. Maybe more."

"He said it wouldn't take longer than twenty or thirty to get here, right?"

"That's what he said, but I'm sure that was just a guess."

My heart was pumping wildly. What would I do if I saw him? Would I even hesitate to put one, or two, or ten into his chest? I wouldn't know until I saw him.

Five more minutes passed and still nothing. I shuffled in place and couldn't get comfortable. Something felt off.

"What did you see on the map?" I had to know.

"There was only one way here. Mathis couldn't have avoided coming through here, not if he intended to reach the harbor," Kill said.

I sighed.

"What?" he said.

"Nothing, it's just . . ."

"Just what?" he said.

"I've got a feeling he isn't coming this way."

"Where else would he go?"

"Pull up that map again," I said.

Kill lifted his phone, found his GPS, then zoomed in on the picture of the river.

"There." I pointed to an inlet. It was blocked from our

view on the bridge but wasn't far from Mr. Winston's property. "That's where he went in."

"How can you be sure?" Kill said. "Lyons said you knew him best. Said that he loved boats. The ocean. That he would do anything to get back to the sea and flee the country."

"He would, but not like this. He's not gonna go out in a canoe. Where would that get him?"

"What about what Lyons said? Said he would double back to the marina. Try and steal another vessel. Maybe even get back the one he stole from Orange Beach?"

"C'mon, Kill, you really think the police haven't impounded that yacht by now? No way he's going back there. He needs to lay low—at least until dark. Hell, that's what I'd do. Who knows? He may have been shot." I was speculating, but I had to look at this from all the angles.

"I don't think so. If Winston shot him with a scatter gun, we'd have been picking up pieces of Mathis on his property," Kill said.

"Look, I'll I'm saying is, it's possible. You can stay here if you want, but I'm checking that inlet."

I turned and started walking back to the squad car. As I did, the police helicopter flew overhead. At the sight of the chopper, I diverted my path back to the officer who was directing traffic.

"Excuse me," I said.

"What is it?"

"Can you patch into that chopper's radio?"

The officer looked to the sky. "Check with Jerry over there." He rolled his head behind him.

I walked toward Jerry and asked the same question.

"Sure can. What do you need?"

"Ask him if has eyes on any green canoes. It might be pushed ashore."

Jerry did as he was asked. The radio fell silent for a moment, then the pilot came back. "Nothing yet, sir."

I gritted my teeth. "There's an inlet about 1,500 feet back and around the bend. Can you tell him to concentrate his search area there?"

Jerry nodded and relayed the information.

"Roger that," the pilot said.

I watched the chopper head in that direction. Just as it turned, Kill walked over. "What's going on?"

"I asked the chopper pilot to head toward the inlet. See if he can see anything from the sky."

Kill didn't say anything. He just waited for an answer.

We could see the chopper hovering there. Moving forward in small increments.

"We can't see anything, not from the sky, there's too much tree coverage. You'll need to access the area from the street," the pilot said.

"Thank you." I nodded to Jerry, then turned.

Kill jogged in from behind me. "Looks like you were right," he said.

I nodded.

Then he added, "But I'd feel like a real asshole if we both went to check it out and somehow Mathis escaped the police here."

I looked back at the roadblock. "No one's getting through that."

"You say that now, but you've said it yourself, local police have screwed up in the past. Do you really want to leave him in their hands?"

I was at a loss. How could Mathis still come? There was

no way. But Kill had put that doubt in my head. Put the question of *what if*.

"So, what's your thought then. Stay here?" I said.

"One of us should."

"Go on then, head back to the bridge." I spun and started walking again.

He grabbed my arm and said, "No. I should check out the inlet."

"What? Why?"

"Thirty-five years of chasing down bad guys who flee, that's why."

"So, that's it, you don't trust me?" Rage boiled over. How could he even think that?

"Look, I don't wanna say it, but you haven't had the best track record at chasing him down by yourself. Look where it got you last time. In the hospital. Maybe this time it will be the morgue."

"Screw you, asshole." I ripped my arm from his grasp. I didn't need to stand there and listen to him judge me for my decisions. Even if he had a point, I just didn't want to listen to it.

"I'm not asking," Kill said.

"So what? You're ordering me now?"

"I didn't want to pull rank on you, but yes."

I huffed again and looked back toward the bridge.

"Hey. Hey." There was some commotion and then the police gathered in the middle of the bridge. "I . . . I think we've got something here," one of the officers said.

I looked at Kill but didn't wait for him to come along. "Or maybe he'll come right to us." I grinned and ran to meet that bastard head on.

It wasn't fear anymore that I felt, but jubilation. Mathis

was heading right toward us, and there was nothing he could do. There was no escape he could make, not in a canoe.

Five of us stood on the bridge, each with our guns outstretched and ready to fire. Problem was, there was nothing to fire at. The boat floating toward us wasn't a canoe, but a kayak. Blaze orange and most definitely not Mathis.

The person paddling the boat was a thin woman in a bikini. Startled, she saw us and immediately threw up her hands.

"Excellent police work, boys." I mocked, then raised my gun and looked back in search of Kill. But he wasn't there. He was gone, and so was the squad car we'd arrived in.

28

I WALKED AWAY FROM THE HORDE OF OFFICERS WHO STOOD idly by and offered their apologies to the woman who paddled underneath the bridge and out into the bay.

As I stared at the empty space where the squad car Kill took had been, I felt a vibration in my pocket. *That's him, gotta be. You better have a damn good explanation for yourself.* But it wasn't Deputy Kill, it was Billy.

"Billy, what's up?" I played dumb. I wanted to see what he said.

"Mathis isn't at the hotel."

"I know."

"What do you mean? Do you have him?" Billy's voice rose, like he was excited, not bummed.

"Uh, no, but . . ." I stalled, trying to figure his excitement. Wouldn't he be concerned? Or tell me more ways on how to stop pursuing Mathis? If he was truly guilty, wouldn't he make up some excuse for me to come down there?

"But what? Tell me," he urged.

Mathis wasn't coming to the bridge. I didn't know why I

needed to tell myself again. But I needed a car to make for the inlet and help Kill.

"Can you get up here or are you still at the hotel?"

"No," Billy said.

"No to what? You can't get here or you're not at the hotel?" I was surprised.

"I'm on the boat. The one Mathis stole from Orange Beach."

"The boat?" I said, then realized, that was perfect. "Can you take it?"

"What? The boat?" Billy said.

"No, the RV. Yes. Of course the boat."

"Take it where?"

"Here."

"Where's here?"

"North of your location. Up the intracoastal, there's a waterway that connects to the bay. If we can take the boat further downstream, we might be able to see where Mathis went ashore."

"What do you mean went ashore?" Billy's voice was stern. Now he sounded more irritated than excited. "You found out where he was, and you didn't tell me?"

I dropped my head. I still couldn't be certain Billy wasn't playing me, but from his reaction to Mathis, it sounded more like he wasn't helping Mathis at all.

"We found a spot where Mathis stole a canoe."

"Where?"

"A few blocks away from the house with the pink scooter."

Billy waited on his end. "So . . . he was there? You *were* right."

"Technically, I think Kill was right, but yeah . . . it was

his intel that led us to the house in the first place."

Billy spoke again, but I didn't hear what he said next. "Wait." I cut him off. "How did Kill know?" I thought out loud.

Billy answered my question. "He said he had a contact within DOT. Told him the traffic cams followed the pink scooter to the street."

I didn't hesitate to ask my next question. "Did you see any traffic cams? Honestly, I didn't even look, I just took his word for it."

"No, I didn't check either—Jasper, what are you thinking?"

"Sonofabitch," I said to myself.

"Jasper? Jasper?" Billy said.

"Hold on, Billy." I held the phone to my chest and walked toward the gathered policemen. "Do you guys have traffic cameras set up in the neighborhoods around here?"

They all looked to each other and each shook their heads no. Then one said, "Only near the causeway. Nothing around here."

I gulped. Then got back on the phone with Billy. "It was Kill," I told him.

"What was Kill?" Billy had no idea what I was on to.

"He's in on it with Mathis," I said.

"In on what—Jasper, what the hell are you talking about?"

"Kill and Mathis are in conspiring together."

Silence lingered on the other end until Billy came through again. "You're shitting me. There's no way."

"Think about it," I said, then spun to ask if I could borrow a car. All the officers looked to me with blank stares. "Any car. Now."

"Take mine." An officer flipped me the keys. "It's that one there." He pointed to the opposite end of the bridge.

I ran toward the vehicle when Billy spoke. "James, what the hell are you doing?"

"Sorry, Billy, I can't wait for you. I need to go after them."

"James, wait, I'll come pick you up. We can go together," Billy said, but I couldn't. They'd be long gone by the time he got there.

"Sorry, Billy, I can't."

"Damnit, Jasper. You know what happened last time. And now there's two of them. I don't want to bury you this week. Just wait for me. I'm on my way."

I dropped the phone from my ear and heard his continuous pleas and cries.

"Jasper, at least tell me where you're going," he said, then I hung up my phone and slumped into the squad car.

Sitting in the front seat, I studied my route on the map. The search area was small—only a couple city blocks surrounded that inlet. But Kill and Mathis had a huge head start. I didn't know what I'd find, if anything. But I'd be damned if they were going to outwit me and make me out to be the fool. I had to try. Even if it was a massive mistake.

29

Ever since Mathis sent the text message, he was light-headed and found it difficult to stand or move for an extended period. So when someone grabbed the handle of the front door, he hoped the person there was his ally and not the homeowner.

Then he realized, no homeowner would use the front door, not when they had access through the garage. Then came a knock. Mathis staggered to his feet and stumbled down the hallway while reaching for the walls to stabilize himself.

He wiped his fingers across the old wallpaper. He didn't notice right away, not until he came close to the door, but his hand left a trail of blood along the wall.

Mathis didn't bother to look around the glass to identify the person knocking, he didn't have the time nor strength to care.

He opened the door and saw a man standing there. Mathis forced a smile and said, "About time you showed up."

Deputy Kill pushed inside and walked beyond him. Kill didn't bother helping him into the kitchen. Mathis let the door slam, then followed his own trail of blood back down the hallway. When he arrived in the kitchen, Kill was standing with his back to him.

"Are you going to call an ambulance?" Mathis said.

"I think you and I both know that's not an option."

Mathis' head fell. "What then? Stay here until I bleed to death."

Mathis' fate was sealed.

"That's not my concern. Once I get what I came here for, I don't care what you do."

"What you came here for?" Mathis felt his body give out when he fell into a chair at the nearby table.

Finally Kill spun around and bent to his level. He pounded the table with both fists. "Don't play dumb with me, Archibald. Where are they? Where are the diamonds?"

Mathis swallowed. One of the last jobs Mathis had done before finding himself cornered at the Jacksonville Port Authority was a jewelry heist.

The job wasn't as mindless as holding up a local jewelry store in the mall . . . No, Mathis had gone directly to the source of the diamonds in Russia. Not many authorities in the United States even knew about the heist—including Jasper James. One of the only ones who did was Deputy Jack Kill. When the job was done and Mathis returned to the United States, Kill hadn't been able to reach him, not until things cooled off. But Mathis hadn't allowed things to cool off. Instead he'd put two bullets into Agent James' chest.

Mathis licked his lips and shrugged his shoulders, then said, "I don't remember."

Kill lifted his fists from the table, then slammed them into Mathis' thigh. Even though he didn't puncture the wounds on the backside of his leg, the hit was excruciating, and Mathis let out a tormented roar.

Mathis struggled to push Kill off. He was too strong. Kill had to be careful though, he couldn't have Mathis pass out and never wake again.

"Where are they?" Kill gnashed his teeth.

"I'm never going to tell. If I die, you'll never find them."

Kill stood over Mathis, doing his best to intimidate. "Then maybe I'll pay a visit to your lady friend in New Orleans. Ask her if she knows where my diamonds are. Bleed her for information."

Mathis lurched for him like he was shot from a canon. As he did, Kill stepped aside, and Mathis fell to the unforgiving ground.

From the wood floor, Mathis peered up and said, "You wouldn't. She's innocent in this. This is between you and me. There's no need to get her involved."

"You got her involved when you led the FBI right to her."

Mathis' mouth hung open. "What do you mean? How? How did they find her?"

Kill shook his head back and forth and chuckled in his own amusement. "Archie, you really are a bleeding heart, aren't you?"

"What do you mean?"

"James found the picture when he was rifling through your old files. Something they picked up on a prior bust. How else do you think they've been able to track you all the way down here? James found her in New Orleans. Pressed her for information."

"She gave me up?" Mathis sounded surprised.

"Of course she gave you up. Led us right to the jughead bodybuilders."

"No . . . she . . . she wouldn't do that."

"I assure you, she did."

"Cleo? Why?" Mathis was in disbelief.

"Because she didn't love you the way you loved her."

That was a shot to his heart.

All the air left Mathis lungs as he laid there.

"Now prove it," Kill said.

"Prove what?"

"How much you loved her. Tell me where the diamonds are or she gets two to the chest, just like you gave Special Agent James. Call it cruel irony." Kill certainly did have a flare for the dramatic.

Mathis drew in breath, then pushed it out.

"And if you wouldn't mind, I'm in a bit of a hurry because Special Agent James will be walking through that door at any moment."

"Then why wouldn't I wait?" Mathis said. "Tell him everything. About you. Me. About the operations we've pulled together over the years. About the real reason he's never been able to catch me."

"You really think he's gonna take your word for it? That ship has sailed. You shot him in the chest twice. He's itching to put you down. I wouldn't be able to protect you. You'd be dead before you could even try to convince him otherwise."

There was a pause. Then Mathis said, "If I tell you, you swear to me Cleo stays untouched?"

"Promise you that," Kill said.

Then a smile formed on Mathis' face. He thought of

something, something he could do for Cleo. One last gift to give her.

"What about her brother?" Mathis said.

"What about him?"

"You get him out of prison."

"How am I gonna do that? Once I leave this room, my life in the government is all but over. James doesn't know my connection with you yet, but he'll figure it out soon enough. I won't be able to show my face again. I need the diamonds to disappear."

"As you stated earlier, not my concern. I'm sure you still have some connections. Someone that owes you a favor. Isn't that how law enforcement works? Bend the rules for your own benefit?"

"No. I—" Kill started.

"Do it, or I won't give the diamonds up."

"Fine. I'll find a way." Kill didn't hesitate.

"How will I know you'll stick to your word?"

"You won't."

"Then I need insurance." Mathis lifted his phone from his pocket and began to type in a name before texting.

"What are you doing?" Kill walked forward to try and see.

"Adding insurance."

"What the hell does that mean?"

Mathis kept texting. "It means I'm texting my contact with the diamonds. She has the location and now instructions with the only way you can collect."

"How will I contact her?"

"You won't. She'll contact you once Cleo's brother is a free man. From there, you'll be given the diamonds. Do we have a deal?"

"Deal," Kill said.

"Good." Mathis continued to text until he was satisfied with his instructions. "Now get on with it. I'm starting to run cold, and I don't want to bleed out on this floor any longer. I've accepted I'm going to die. Now that I know Cleo will be safe, I'm ready."

Kill walked over to the couch to grab a throw pillow. After returning to Mathis, he brought the pillow to the end of the muzzle of his Glock and placed it over Mathis' face.

After the deed was done, Kill stepped over Mathis' lifeless body, and walked out the front door like nothing had happened.

30

ACCORDING TO THE MAP, THERE WAS A SMALL BRIDGE JUST ahead. I kept a lookout for another squad car, but there were none in sight—at least not on the street I drove on. The street was narrow and felt claustrophobic. No cars were parked on the sides of the road, which I found a little odd— until I saw the *No Parking* signs that hung on both sides.

There was a small break in the trees ahead of me. That had to be the river. I lifted my foot off the gas and slowed to a crawl. From inside the car, I couldn't see it yet, but from the looks of it, the clearance from the surface of the water to the bottom of the bridge couldn't have been more than two to three feet.

I studied the rearview mirror to make sure no one was coming, then grabbed my cell and texted Billy the exact location.

When I stepped out of the car, I walked to the edge on the west side of the bridge and peered over. It was about an eight-foot drop. The water was clear. It couldn't have been deeper than two feet.

After moving to the opposite side of the bridge, I contorted my body so I could see through the dense trees and the snaking river that wound around the corner. Something was there. Stuck inside the brush about 100 yards from the road.

A boat was pulled ashore, but I couldn't tell if it was a canoe.

There was a concrete barrier to the right of the bridge, and that was where I jumped down from the road and onto the shoreline. Once on shore, I lifted my Glock and proceeded slowly.

The shore wasn't wide, maybe a foot from the edge of the brush to the water. Tree limbs stuck out like long bending arms and scratched me as I passed.

As I came closer to the boat, I looked up toward the sky but couldn't see through the branches and leaves. "No wonder the chopper couldn't see anything," I said to myself.

When I looked down again, I went rigid. My path was cut off by a swimming water snake. I hate snakes. The snake slithered through the water about ten feet in front of me.

The snake wasn't venomous, but I pointed my Glock directly at him in case he decided to take a run at me. Problem was though, if I fired a round, I'd alert everyone in the area, and I could scare off Mathis and Kill—if they were even still around. Luckily, the snake caught the edge of the opposite side and disappeared into the neighboring yard.

I let go of the breath I was holding in and continued walking, but more carefully now. A thick tree branch jutted into the water and it was unavoidable. I walked around the limb—fueled forward by what I saw just beyond the branch.

A green canoe.

But was it the canoe that Mathis stole?

When I got close, I saw something I didn't expect. The bottom of the canoe was full of blood.

Wait, was Mathis shot?

I stared for only a moment because my cell phone vibrated in my pocket. It was Billy.

"Hello," I whispered.

"Where the hell are you?" he shouted into the phone.

"Follow the directions and you'll see the squad car parked over the bridge."

"Are you waiting for me?"

"No. I found the abandoned canoe."

"Where?"

"About 100 yards upstream from the car."

"Any sign of Mathis?"

"No, but there's blood. A lot of blood." I looked back into the canoe. If it was his, he wasn't getting much farther. Not without a transfusion.

"Blood? What do you mean, blood?" Billy was surprised. "Is it Mathis'?"

"Can't tell, but I'm about to find out."

"No. Wait."

"Can't. If this is his blood, he's not gonna last much longer. He'll either need a hospital or a morgue depending on the timing. Just hurry and follow the signs. I'll call back if I see anything else."

I hung up on him and noticed a path toward a house. Pushing the tree branches aside, I followed the path.

Watching where I stepped, because of that stupid water snake, I saw where the grass had been pushed down by something. Maybe a dragging foot—I couldn't be certain—

but aside from the grass, there was some staining. I bent down to make sure I wasn't seeing things. I wasn't. Blood stained the grass.

I snapped my head up and looked back at the house. Mathis was there, I knew it. But still there was no sign of Kill or the squad car. He had to be there too. That was the exact river we saw on his phone's GPS.

Standing at the back door of the house, I reached for the screen. Again, there were traces of blood. There was also a window, just to the right. I stepped toward it. It was about at chest height. Standing against the siding, I peeked inside. There was no movement—no voices coming from inside.

But when I looked closer, I saw something leading away from the kitchen and toward the front door: a trail of bloody fingerprints on the wall.

I rushed back toward the screen, opened it, and walked inside. My heart was in my throat at that moment, but it didn't take long for me to see a man lying on the floor. I skipped over him to clear the house first—the last thing I needed was to be surprised by the perpetrator hiding in a closet or bathroom.

No one was there—not inside or out. After running out the front door in search of Kill or the squad car, I came back and holstered my Glock.

Standing over the body, I looked down. There was a flower-printed throw pillow over the man's face with a bullet hole through the center. My stomach fell as I looked down at the man's legs. The backs of his legs were bleeding as well.

When I lifted the pillow, my chin dropped to my chest. It was Mathis. He'd been executed. Sure, he may have died from blood loss anyhow, but it looked like Kill wanted to make a statement.

"Why?" I asked Mathis' dead body. "What did he have on you?"

I couldn't figure it out. Why was Kill working with him? What would a US Marshal and a thief have to gain by working together?

Of course, I knew the answer. Anyone in my position would know the answer. They were scoring the jobs together. Kill would keep law enforcement at bay while Mathis would come up with plans and they'd split the profits equally.

I just couldn't believe it. My phone buzzed in my pocket. Billy called again.

I didn't even say hello, "Mathis is dead."

"What? How?"

"Kill."

"What do you mean? Kill shot him?"

"No. I mean Kill executed him."

There was silence on the other end. "Woah, what?"

"I told you they were working together."

"What evidence do you have?"

"Aside from the dead man I'm standing over?"

"Yeah, aside from that? What if Kill had to shoot him? Maybe Mathis attacked him and he had no choice."

Of course, Billy would ask that. He hadn't witnessed the scene I was witnessing.

"Just wait until you get here. Then I'll let you form your own opinion of what happened."

I walked to the kitchen table where there was a stack of mail and read off the address so Billy could come.

Then I walked back over to Mathis' body. I stared at him

for the better part of three minutes. Deep down, I wanted to be the one who captured or killed him. But part of me was relieved I didn't have to do either. The other part of me was spurred on to a new goal. Tracking down Kill and making sure he got what he deserved.

31

BILLY ARRIVED ABOUT THE SAME TIME AS THE AMBULANCE AND the local police. They had a lot of questions for me. Honestly though, I was only half paying attention to their questions because my concern was how we would track down Deputy Kill. Where was he gonna go? No way he could show his face around the US Marshal's office. I didn't have the proof I needed that he killed Mathis, but he was nowhere to be found and his cell phone went straight to voicemail—that made it clear he was on the run.

How was I—or anyone for that matter—going to track down a man who was trained by the US government to do exactly what he was trying to avoid? That manhunt was going to take every resource possible. But knowing Cohen —and the higher ups in the FBI—they would consider the situation my fault once again.

When Billy finished giving his statement to the local police, he met me as I rested my tired legs on the back of a squad car.

"What now?" he said.

I looked at him. I needed to get something off my chest —something I locked inside. I owed him that much. "Billy, I need to apologize."

"For what?" he reached into his pocket for a pack of smokes.

"I thought you gave those things up." I didn't want to come clean and that was the best place to stall for a moment.

Through his closed mouth that locked the cigarette in place, he said, "I did." He grinned, then lit it and took a draw. "So, what's with the apology?"

My tongue felt glued to the roof of my mouth. Aside from being my best friend, he was my family. How could I have even questioned him?

Sinful human nature, I supposed.

"I . . . I thought you were the one who was working with Mathis."

He stepped away from the bumper and squared his chest to mine. His gaze was unyielding, and he pulled his mouth tight, like his words were about to tear at me with the strike of his tongue. But instead of inflicting me with an upheaval of humiliation, he smiled, and said, "Nah, not enough money in the world could get me to turn on you."

I felt . . . a sudden rush of admiration for him.

"What? Really? That's it? You're not pissed?"

"Oh, I'm pissed, but it's not the money I'd be after. It's the thrill of the hunt. And I don't want to hunt you. I pity you. I mean you're kinda pathetic. You let some jewel thief shoot you in the chest twice. Come on, what is that? You can't even call it a rookie mistake cause we're far from rookies."

"Shut up." I nudged him with my shoulder.

"Nah, man, if I was working with Mathis, I would've trained him better. Go for the head shot after you get two in the chest. Only a broken-down Marshal would leave out that critical information."

Billy kept taking pulls on his cigarette. I looked at him and grinned. I could've gone for one myself.

After we shared our laughs, Billy said, "So . . . like I said, what's next?"

"We go after the old man."

"That sounds well and good, but do you have any idea where to start? I know Cohen isn't gonna be happy with all this."

"Why not? We got our guy." I nodded to the stretcher that Mathis was being wheeled out on directly into the back of the ambulance. "Check one off the Top Ten list."

"Yeah, but we let another get away. I'm sure she's gonna put more onus on the rat inside the Marshal's office than Mathis."

"Hey, as far as I'm concerned, she let him in. He was waiting in her office when we came to her with the Cleo theory."

"Do you think she's in on it too?" I said.

"What? No way?" Billy said. "Not Cohen."

"Why not?" Of course, I didn't have proof. "She did show up at the hospital right away. How did she get there so quick? Was she on her way down with you?"

I could see it in Billy's eyes. He was thinking about it.

"No," he said. "But you were in surgery for a while. I know she got on the first flight from Atlanta."

"If you say so," I said. I didn't have any proof she was in on the action with Mathis and Deputy Kill, but I was just saying, wouldn't that have been a punch to the gut. Or more likely, a kick to the balls.

"What were her instructions when you gave her the news?" Billy said.

"Come back to Jacksonville."

"She's still there? I figured she'd head back to Atlanta."

"Apparently not."

"Are we going back?" he said.

I was taken back. "What? You want to defy her order?"

"If you think she's really dirty, why not go after Kill ourselves? Vigilante style." Billy grinned through the puff of smoke.

For a second, I thought about it. Then realized, if Cohen was dirty, I—no, we—needed proof. And going after Kill in Clearwater wasn't gonna net us an arrest. He was too smart to stick around. He had friends—maybe on our side of the law and the other to help him. We needed a strategy. And I needed time to think about my next move.

"I think we head back to Jacksonville. Retrace our steps and see what Cohen has for us. She was clear on the call. Plus, she said she had something new—something to break the case wide open."

"What news?" Billy said.

"No idea. She wouldn't tell me."

"Maybe it's bullshit."

I chuckled. "Yeah maybe. Why don't we wait until she gives us the new information? Then make our judgements."

"So on to Jacksonville then?" Billy rose from the car and flicked his cigarette away.

"On to Jacksonville." I nodded and followed him.

32

COHEN MET US AT THE AIRPORT. FRANKLY, I WAS A LITTLE surprised to see her, but apparently the information she had couldn't wait until we got to the federal building.

"What's she doing here?" Billy said as we deplaned. I was about to tell him my thoughts, but then he leaned over and said, "You still think she's dirty?"

I eyed her. On the plane ride over, I'd had time to think —to mull over my reaction to Billy, Mathis, Kill, and Cohen. There was no way. She couldn't have hidden that from us.

"I mean look at her." I watched Billy eye her. "If that isn't the quintessential look of a rat, I don't know what is."

I couldn't tell if he was serious—even as well as I knew him, I still couldn't tell.

"About time you two got back here," Cohen said from far off, but loud enough for us to hear her annoyed tone.

"We came as soon as we were summoned," I said.

"Yeah, came to get this 'new' information you've got for us," Billy added with a grin.

"What's with the air-quoted emphasis on the 'new' information?" she said.

"No, I, uh . . ." Billy backtracked.

"Come on, spit it out, Lyons. What you think, I've been sitting on this information for a long time?"

"No, it's not—" Billy started but she cut him off.

"Well, it's either that or you don't understand how to use air quotes. Both scenarios don't bode well for you."

"Sheesh, somebody's in a mood today," I stood up for Billy.

"Can it, James."

Her tone was harsh. Clearly, she had a problem, but I couldn't understand why until she said, "It's been confirmed that Deputy Jack Kill was working with Archibald Mathis. They pulled multiple jobs over the years."

I nudged Billy and said, "See." Out of the side of my mouth.

"So you knew the entire time?" Cohen said.

Even before I could answer, she threw her hands up in disgust. "Damnit, James that makes this whole thing even worse."

"I didn't know exactly, it was just a feeling."

"Well, you should've listened to that feeling earlier on. Apparently Kill and Mathis have been playing the system for quite a long time. Obviously, we only found out now, but stuff has been coming down from the top—from the powers that be in the Marshal Service. The information on Mathis and Kill was classified—even above my pay grade. They pulled one last job together—a diamond heist in Russia."

Russia? What the hell? "How much did they get?"

"Millions in uncut diamonds," she said.

"And what do you mean, classified?" Billy added.

"I mean, he was inserted onto my team for a reason. But even I wasn't given the reason until I received the information I'm giving you now."

"That's bogus. Why would the Marshal Service insert him into our team and risk our lives?"

"That's a question for another day. But the only response the director gave me was they needed to see how Kill would react—what he would do once he got close to Mathis. The Marshal service thinks Mathis didn't pull his end of the Russian job."

"What do you mean?" I said.

"For some reason, they think the diamonds are hidden somewhere. That's why Kill wanted onto the task force so bad. To find a way to get Mathis alone and extract the intelligence from his partner."

I couldn't believe it, but if what Cohen was saying was true, everything that had taken place made complete sense.

"So they were willing to put us all in danger?" Billy was stuck on what the Marshal service did.

"It seems that way," Cohen said.

"That's bullshit," Billy said.

"Tell me about it," she said.

"That's why you're pissed, isn't it?" I said.

"What do you mean?" Cohen said.

"You're not mad at us, you're just deflecting your anger. Letting your emotions get the best of you," I said.

"Whoa, easy, Dr. Freud," Cohen said.

"Looks like someone's been listening during those therapy sessions, huh?" Billy chuckled. "Here I just thought those sessions were a way to check a box, not that you'd find the inner you."

"Nope. I found the inner me a long time ago. I'm just

saying, you know, she seems a little tense." Billy and I were trying to lighten the mood.

"Oh, will both of you just shutup," she said.

"Well, you did think she was a rat," Billy nudged me.

Cohen fell silent. I looked at Billy with wide eyes. The bastard had ripped my guts out with one sentence.

"What?" He shrugged, then leaned in, and whispered, "Payback for suspecting me."

"Excuse me?" Cohen put her hands on her hips and leaned forward, almost getting nose to nose. "What the hell is he talking about?"

"I'll just be standing over here and enjoying the show," Billy slipped in before he walked away.

She watched Billy, but anyone could tell she was pissed only at me. I needed to choose my next words carefully.

"I . . . I, uh, we—"

"Stop stammering like a fool and give it to me straight," Cohen said.

"I thought maybe, you were, uh, in on it, you know with Mathis and Kill."

Her eyes were as big as olives, and she gritted her teeth.

Like a bumbling idiot, I continued. "You know because Kill was in your office at the time we showed up with the photograph of Cleo from New Orleans."

In her seething anger, she said, "He was inserted into our team." She hammered that point home.

"Oh, I know, I know, it's just, me and Billy, we were just thinking out loud. I mean, I'm sorry, it . . . it won't happen again."

"Bad things happen to you when you think, don't they, James?"

I needed to make things right. "You're right, you're right, I'm sorry."

She was flustered, and I could see she wanted to say something else. I needed to stand my ground and take it like a man. Atone for my sins.

But she didn't take out any further anger on me. The only thing left to say was, "Take Lyons and get out my sight."

We scooted away from her, and as we walked, I said out of the side of my mouth, "You bastard."

He was laughing so hard he almost fell over. But when he finally came to, he said, "You deserved it."

And I did.

33

I STARED AT THE BLINKING CURSOR ON MY COMPUTER AND couldn't think about what to include in my report on the Mathis case. Something continued to dig into my side like a dull knife. The scene at JAXPORT kept on playing over in my mind. Up until that point, all I remembered seeing was the smoke blowing from the end of Mathis' gun. But the more I thought—whilst I stared at an unwritten page—was him. Only Mathis.

Billy spied me from his desk and leaned in his chair. "What?" He could tell I was deep in thought.

I didn't answer. I couldn't, because right then I remembered. Mathis had a black backpack slung around his arm at the airport.

"Bastard," I muttered to myself.

"What?" Billy asked again.

I had no answer for him: I needed more facts. There were pictures of Mathis sitting at the gate in the airport sent over from the Department of Homeland Security. The files were on my computer in an unlocked folder. I clicked on the first picture and it was clear as day.

"Sonofabitch."

Billy stood behind me, peering over my shoulder at the computer screen. "What are we looking at?"

I leaned in my chair and spun around to face him. "Mathis at the airport."

"O . . . kay," Billy said. "What about him?"

"Do you see the backpack?"

Billy leaned in closer. "Yeah sure."

"He had the same one at JAXPORT."

Billy scrunched his brow. "But I thought you couldn't remember anything?"

"I couldn't." I kept scrolling through the rest of the pictures. "Not until now."

Billy continued to stand and said, "You think that's the bag Cohen was talking about? You think he had the diamonds with him the entire time?"

I jumped from my chair and looked square in Billy's eyes. "I don't think—I know those were the diamonds. You heard her, that's why Kill was so pissed. I bet you anything Mathis hid them from him."

"You think he ditched the bag at JAXPORT? Why would he do that? He had to know he'd never get back there, especially after he shot you."

"I don't know, Billy, but we gotta go check." I didn't even wait for him, I just grabbed my jacket and walked away from the desk.

Billy caught me from behind me spoke truth. "James, stop." He grabbed my arm.

"What?"

"Think about it. If he ditched the backpack there, those

crates would've been shipped somewhere in the world. Mathis wouldn't drop the stash there, it's stupid."

Billy was right. But I couldn't let it go, not until I checked for myself. So I made up some other reason to go. "What if he stashed the bag somewhere else? Somewhere around the area. Not in a crate."

"He wouldn't have had the time. You said it yourself. You saw him with the backpack around his back before he shot you, right?"

"Yeah, so?"

"Then, there you go. He wouldn't have had the time to search around for somewhere safe to drop it. Trust me, James, the bag's not there."

Billy made his point again, and I knew he was right. "So what, where do you think he brought it?"

"I don't know, Jasper, but I guarantee it's not at JAXPORT."

"Do whatever you want, I'm going to check."

Billy sighed, then looked in my eyes. "You know I'm going with you."

"Well, alright then, let's go." I turned and started walking toward the elevator doors. "Bet you twenty bucks we find the backpack hidden."

"You're on," he said as we waited for the elevator door to open. "I'll take your money."

I COULDN'T BELIEVE the number of cars and shipping containers around the area as we drove into JAXPORT. I knew there was no way I would remember where Mathis shot me, especially since everything had been moved since the last time I was there.

We called ahead and asked a customs agent to meet us when we arrived.

"How y'all doing?" he said when we stepped out of the car. "Cal Dotson," he said.

"James and Lyons," I said.

"James?" Dotson said. "You're the one who got shot then, huh?"

Thrown, I said, "Uh, yeah, that's me."

"Huh, cool." He nodded to himself.

"Right." I tried to move past the nonsensical comments. "Would you be able to show us back to the scene?" Customs had to know exactly where it was, even if I didn't have the recollection.

"Of course." He insisted we load into the golf cart he had sitting behind him. "Hop in."

The golf cart had two seats. One was a bench seat across the front like any other golf cart, but the backside also had a bench seat facing the opposite direction. I let Billy have the front to avoid any further embarrassing questions about how I let somebody shoot me in the chest.

As Dotson drove, I took in the sights. Maroon and blue shipping containers were stacked to the sky. On one row I counted at least five stacked on top of each other. I wondered what was in them.

"What's in these things?" Billy asked. It seemed we shared a brain.

"Oh, you, know, this and that. Packages. Produce. Alcohol. Bit of everything."

"And they go all over the world?" Billy asked.

"Yep," he said.

What if Mathis did drop the backpack there? What if he came to JAXPORT intentionally? Maybe JAXPORT was planned from the beginning. No. That doesn't make sense. Not really. He was about to board a plane.

As we drove, my stomach squeezed like a vice. Was I really going back to the scene? With every turn, I dreaded the memory that would come next. I couldn't calm my breathing when the anxiety struck. I was having a panic attack on the back of a golf cart. Billy didn't know it. Dotson didn't know it. But I did. I sucked my breath in deep, but my vision was starting to blur. *Don't pass out*, I told myself. *Keep it together.*

Then the cart stopped. "Here we are." Dotson jumped down from the driver's seat.

I closed my eyes, then took another breath.

"Jasper, you alright?" Billy said and walked toward me.

"Fine." I rose from the backseat. "Let's do this," I had to say to pump myself up.

Dotson led us down the corridor of stacked shipping containers. They walled the walkway, towering over us. I swore they were leaning, closing in on me. But that was just insecurity seeping through.

"We found you down here," Dotson said.

"Who found me? You?" I didn't know why I was mad at him, but my tone was harsh.

"No. Not me. Agent Jackson, he's off today."

"How did Mathis stand to escape?" Billy said.

I looked to Dotson. "Yeah, seriously."

"By the time we heard the shots, he'd stolen another vehicle and made a break for it. We had no idea he was even here, not until it was too late. No one informed us."

My heart sank. "Yeah, that was my fault. I got cocky. Thought I could take him out myself."

"That was stupid," Dotson said.

Wow. Direct. I wasn't used to that. Especially not when it came to joking about my life.

"Sorry, I didn't mean to sound insensitive. I say things sometimes. You know, without thinking," Dotson said.

"Happens to the best of us," Billy said.

He was right, it was stupid. I walked beyond both, toward a dead end where the shipping containers touched perpendicularly.

"What?" Billy yelled out.

I didn't say anything, not until I walked back toward them. "Mathis had a backpack with him."

"Okay?" Dotson said.

"Nothing has been recovered has it?" I said.

"Depends. What's in it?" Dotson chuckled to himself.

I wasn't in a joking mood and the answer was above his pay grade. I didn't want to offend him or insult him, so I thought about what to say. But before I could speak, Billy did first, "We don't know for sure."

Nice. It wasn't exactly a lie.

"No. Nothing has been recovered. Not that I know of. And as you're aware, your guys combed the entire shipping yard after you were shot." He pointed to me.

"What about the Marshal Service?"

"What about them?"

He looked toward the ground to recall. "Um, yeah, yeah." He nodded up and down. "I met a guy. Said he was from the Marshal Service. His name was, uh, Kill. Easy to remember a name like that. And the man . . . he was gruff— you know like one of those old cowboy guys in the movies. Like Clint Eastwood, or John Wayne, that sort of thing."

Dotson went on and on.

"Yeah we get it," I said. "What did he want?"

"I don't know. Never told me."

I reeled.

"But he did talk to Jackson," Dotson said.

"The guy who found me?" I said.

"Yeah, yeah," Dotson said.

"Can you call him? Ask him what they talked about?" Billy said.

"Sure, I can try." He stood there a moment looking at us. "You mean, now?"

"Yeah, now," I said.

Dotson lifted his phone, smiled at us, then dialed.

He spun away from Billy and me. Billy came over and said. "Looks like that twenty will be in my hand in . . ." he looked to his watch, ". . . call it, two minutes."

But I didn't pay attention to Billy, I was more interested in Dotson. I watched him. He turned back around and said, "Jackson says he asked about a backpack."

I locked eyes with Billy.

One more piece of the puzzle was falling into place.

34

KILL SAT ON THE METAL BLEACHERS—THE FIRST ROW— staring at an empty baseball field. From under his blue baseball cap, he watched the vacant dirt and imagined an eight-year-old version of himself rounding third and heading for home. There was a smile of joy on his face as he slid into the plate and kicked up a cloud of dust.

But that memory seemed like a lifetime ago. Kill never expected his life to take a turn like it had. But ever since he got in a deep hole with the wrong people, he would have done anything to get himself out of the large gambling debt.

Partnering with Mathis seemed like a logical business agreement—at least in the beginning when the scores were smaller. It was only when the stakes were raised that greed took hold.

Kill had told himself the Russian score was his last job with Mathis before retiring. And he only had a few short years left to work for Uncle Sam before he could buy that boat he wanted and sail off into the sunset.

That dream was gone. At that point, he just wanted to survive the heat.

"Well, I'll be damned. If it isn't Deputy US Marshal Jack Kill," said a man in a very nice Armani suit as he approached.

Kill rose from the metal to meet his old friend. They hugged, and Kill smiled at him but waited to speak.

"So . . ." They took a seat on the bleachers. "Why am I here? What's so important?" the man said.

"I'm in trouble, Mike," Kill said.

"I figured as much. Why else would you call me here of all places?" Mike looked around at the empty park. Kill waited to add more, maybe because he wanted Mike to ask the questions. He was one of the best attorneys in the state of Florida. "What happened? Start from the beginning and don't leave out any details."

"You hear about that Archibald Mathis case?"

"Of course. It's an FBI manhunt case. I figure you and the Marshal Service would be heavily involved."

"We were."

"*Were* being the operative word there. I heard the police found his body in Clearwater," Mike said.

"That's right. In a house."

"Yeah, so."

"So, I put him there."

Mike scrunched his brow. "Tell me it was self-defense."

"Not exactly."

"Not exactly? It either was or it wasn't."

"It wasn't."

Mike ran his fingers through his thinning hair. "What was it then?"

"I suppose it's best if I start from the beginning."

"That is what I asked for," Mike said.

"Mathis and I had been working multiple jobs together over the years."

"Going back how far?" Mike didn't seem surprised at all.

"About twelve years."

Mike drew an annoyed breath this time.

"What do you mean working jobs together?" Mike said, then he took out a Dictaphone, a notepad, and a Montblanc pen.

"You sure that's necessary?"

"For what you're about to tell me . . . yes it is."

Kill rattled off every job he and Mathis had done together, leaving out no detail. Down to how they planned their jobs together, how much money they split each time—everything. He finished with the diamond heist in Russia.

"That's why you killed him? Because of the diamonds?"

"No. Not exactly. He was already going to die from the shotgun wounds, I just expedited the process."

"Why?"

"Because Jasper James—the FBI agent in charge of the manhunt—was on my trail."

"So did you get a response? Did Mathis tell you where the diamonds were?"

"That's where you come in."

"How do you mean?"

"I mean, I need a favor."

"What do you call me meeting with you?"

"Sage advice from an old friend." Kill grinned.

"Oh, sure," Mike said.

"However . . . this favor might take a minor miracle."

"Now you've piqued my interest. What's the favor?"

"I need you to fabricate evidence in a case."

"Which case?"

"A B&E case from early 2015."

"And what does this case have to do with the diamonds' location?"

"It has to do with the man involved in the case. Once he's released from prison, I'll receive a call."

"A call? From whom?"

"No idea. That's just what Mathis told me before—"

"Before what? You put one through his head?"

Kill nodded.

"That's what you have to go on? The word of dying man? Why would he give you his secret? It seems to me he'd take that to the grave just to stick it to you."

"He wouldn't."

"Why not?"

"Because I told him I'd hunt down the only woman in the world he ever loved and put two in her chest."

"You really are a ruthless S.O.B., aren't you?"

Kill didn't respond. He just let the thought ruminate in Mike's mind for a second or two.

"What's the evidence I'll be planting?" Mike asked.

"New evidence in the case that will prove the local PD screwed up and planted evidence at the scene for a quick arrest and conviction."

"Why would anyone buy that?" Mike said.

"Because of this." Kill handed Mike a manila folder.

I SET down a crisp twenty-dollar bill onto Billy's desk. He looked and me and beamed with pride.

"I told you so," he said.

"So you did."

I was about to walk away so I wouldn't have to see him gloat when he asked, "What now?"

I sighed. Where would Kill go? Would he flee the country? Get as far away as possible? One thing we knew for sure . . . Kill was greedy. He murdered Mathis for the diamonds, but we didn't know where he or they were. The best we could hope for was a bit of luck. Some crack in the case where Kill would slip up. Be seen by someone or use a credit card—something we could use to locate him.

I sat down and said, "I don't know."

"You don't know?" Billy said.

But I didn't answer. I couldn't, not while I thought more about Mathis. More about where he had gone after the shooting.

New Orleans.

The city popped into my head. Of course. I scavenged the desk for Cleo Monroe's contact information.

"What are you doing?" Billy saw me throwing everything around.

"Looking for this." I held up the paper with her contact information.

"Great. What's that?"

I didn't say. I simply lifted my phone and dialed. Straight to voicemail. I dialed again. Straight to voicemail.

"What?" Billy knew I had something.

I stared at the paper and didn't tell him, not at first.

"James. What the hell?"

"We gotta go."

I leapt from my seat and grabbed my jacket, then ran to the elevator. Billy followed, and I jammed my thumb into the button when he caught up.

"What's got you frazzled? Where are we going?"

I smiled and said, "New Orleans."

———

"WHAT THIS?" Mike said.

"Incriminating evidence that the local sheriff was being paid off to throw certain cases," Kill said.

"Legit evidence?"

"Who cares? The guy's no longer the sheriff. I actually think he's dead."

Mike grabbed the file and opened it. "Well that works in our favor. The dead can't see, after all." Both shared a chuckle.

Kill shifted his attention onto the field where a father and son had just arrived. The boy couldn't have been older than eight or nine. He carried a bat with him, and the father a bag full of baseballs. The kid ran toward home plate and tapped the end on the plate twice before getting into a crouched batting stance.

From his position on the bleachers, Kill watched the boy swing after his father hurled the first pitch toward him. The boy's swing was effortless. On a perfect plane toward the baseball. The boy connected and sent the baseball skyward, cutting through the air with ease. The ball landed just over second base.

The boy beamed with pride as if he'd just hit a homerun in game seven of the World Series.

Kill didn't hear Mike speak his name. He was lost in the beauty of reminiscing of his own childhood all those years ago, putting himself in the boy's shoes.

"Kill."

He shook himself back to reality.

"I think I might be able to make a case of this. It's going to take a while to process, but if all goes well . . . I think we'll be able to get this case thrown out and make Mr. Monroe a free man."

"You think it's possible?"

"Possible, sure, anything's possible . . . if you know the right laws to break—no, bend—call it a bend of the legal system." Mike winked and nudged him.

"How long until he gets released?"

"Best guess?" Mike curled his lower lip. "Three weeks—a month tops."

"A month? What am I supposed to do for a month? The FBI. The Marshal Service. Hell, every single branch of the government with an acronym will be looking for me."

"I have a safe house."

"Where?"

"Louisiana. North of New Orleans a ways. You can lay low. No one will bother you. It's the kind of town where everybody stays out of each other's business. You're welcome to it as long as this takes."

"You really think this will work?"

"With an ordinary attorney, no. With me, hell yeah."

"You're sure of yourself, aren't you?"

"Would you have called me if I wasn't?"

Kill shook his head no.

"That's what I thought." Mike rose and stretched his arms high to the sky. "Now, c'mon, let's go get a guilty man out of prison."

35

WE DIDN'T TELL COHEN WE WERE GOING TO NEW ORLEANS. It would've taken too long to get approval from the director —especially after our latest blunder. I had a gut feeling about this. Cleo knew something, and Mathis trusted her unequivocally.

I didn't think to tell Duda of our arrival either. I needed a clear head. Plus, I didn't know if I could trust him. Not that he wasn't trustworthy, it's just . . . well, he wasn't seasoned like Billy and me.

Billy drove. He knew exactly where to go. He always had a gift with directions. You could bring the man into a densely covered forest blindfolded, spin him around ten times, and he could still lead you out.

We stopped outside her apartment just as the day waned into the night. "What now?" Billy said, shifting the car into park.

I leaned forward and stared out the windshield. "Let's see how the night plays out."

"You don't want to beat down her door and apply pressure, do you?"

"With her? No. That would only scare her off—she'd seize up and keep the information close to her chest."

Billy turned back on the door. We both watched multiple people pass by on the sidewalk that paralleled her building. College students filtered through like a line during a baseball game, and a few drunk women dressed in bridal apparel stumbled passed too.

"Wish I was going to that party." Billy grinned.

Honestly, I didn't give them a second glance. I was too busy waiting for her to come out. Truth was though, we didn't have confirmation she was there to begin with. It wasn't until the sun faded that we caught our first glimpse of miss Cleo Monroe.

"There." I pointed through the windshield and sat upright.

She was dressed finely in a white V-neck cocktail dress. It had long sleeves, but you could still see the caramel skin on her arms through the lace. She carried a matching white clutch under her arm as well.

"Where's she off to dressed like that?" Billy said.

"No idea."

"Do we follow her?"

"Damn right, we do."

Her car was parked along the sidewalk on the same side as we were and only three cars ahead. She pulled into traffic, and Billy followed her.

She didn't go far. In fact, she drove directly to *Club Indigo*.

"Seriously, a bar?" Billy said, as we pulled over to the side and watched her enter. "Who goes to the bar dressed like that?" Billy said. "Some lucky schmuck is gonna—" I grabbed Billy's arm before he could finish his sentence. He glared at me and said, "What?"

I was leaning forward in my seat, and I could see through the top of the windshield. "Look."

Her name was emblazoned in lights on the sign.

Don't miss it. Tonight only. Cleo Monroe.

"She's got a gig," I said.

"Perfect," Billy said flippantly and threw up his hands. "Now we get to sit out here and wait until closing time."

"Actually, it's perfect."

"What is?" Billy said.

"You wanna go catch a show?" I grinned.

"Thought you'd never ask. 'Bout time the FBI pays me to try to pick up a woman and have a beer on the clock." Billy couldn't mask his enthusiasm.

"The beer, fine. But no woman. Not tonight. Cleo is our objective."

"Sure, Dad," Billy mocked. "I'll be on my best behavior."

When we stepped out of the car, traffic was free flowing. Crossing the street was like playing a game of Frogger. Once we stepped foot on the sidewalk, there was a line extending half a block to pay the cover charge to enter the club.

For half a second, I considered flashing my badge to the bouncer, but then thought better. If we did, we'd have been marked men inside. We couldn't have targets on our backs. I didn't want to draw that kind of attention. I just wanted to observe Cleo. See what kind of woman she was. I didn't know why, honestly. That wasn't normal for me. Not if I knew someone was guilty of a crime. But something about her seemed . . . young—innocent—okay, maybe not inno-cent. Maybe naïve was the right word.

I walked to the end of the line. Billy came close and whispered in my ear, "What are we doing?"

"Waiting in line like everyone else."

"Why? Why not use the power of this bad boy?" Billy held up his wallet.

"Because, I don't want to alarm Cleo. If for some reason she's made aware of our arrival, she might skip out on us. This way, she'll stick around."

"Good thought." Billy took his place behind me in line.

"Got any cash on you?"

"Just the twenty you gave me."

I stared at Billy, and my mouth hung open. "You didn't have the money to pay out from the bet earlier?"

"Nope. Knew I wasn't gonna lose." Billy grinned.

The line moved fast, and when we approached the bouncer at the door, I said, "Give it to me."

"What?"

"The twenty I gave you."

Billy lifted the bill from his pocket and slapped it in my hand. "You still owe me."

With Billy still standing there, I turned over my shoulder and whispered. "Let's play double or nothing."

"What do you have in mind?" Billy said.

"Cleo has the bag."

"What? Here?"

"Here or at her place."

"Not a chance. You're on." Billy shook my hand just as we reached the bouncer.

The bouncer reached out his hand and said, "Forty dollars. And IDs please."

I gave him mine and Billy his.

He scanned over them and handed them back. "Two drink minimum, gentleman." He waved us inside.

Once we were through the front door, the bright lights surprised me at first. They shined down like a spotlight. I had to shield my eyes until we moved further inside. Music from the stereo system blared, and people talked and congregated near the bar or sat at the tables in front of the stage. The room was packed—almost a full house—with only three tables left unattended.

"You get the beers. I'll find the table," I told Billy.

Dodging the masses who stood guzzling their drinks and searching for potential mates, I locked my eyes on an empty table. But it appeared, so had another. A couple walked toward the table—they were closer, but lost in conversation with each other, allowing me to slip underneath them and sit down before either could.

"Bastard," the woman said loud enough for her boyfriend—or whoever he was—to hear.

I didn't care though; I couldn't care. I had to see Cleo perform up close. Again, I didn't know why. Was I really interested? Truth was, she was very attractive. Well . . . as attractive as a woman who helps fugitives go.

I shook that brief momentary lapse in judgment away and told myself I was there to see for myself. To see if she could really be holding the bag full of diamonds we were after.

"Here you go." Billy set my Budweiser down and took the chair next to me. "What time does she go on?"

Before I could even answer, a man walked on stage and grabbed the microphone from the stand. I recognized him as the bartender we'd met when we first arrived in New Orleans with Duda and Deputy Kill.

"Ladies and gentleman." He stood there holding out his hands, trying to calm the rising voices. When most did, he continued. "We've got a very special treat tonight. I want you to give an enormous round of applause for our very own, Cleo Monroe."

Thunderous cheering echoed inside the intimate club. I searched the faces all around. Nothing but joy in every expression. Clearly, she was good, or at least well-respected.

I turned my attention away from the crowd and back on the stage. When she walked out, the air was sucked from my lungs. She stood in the same dress we watched her leave her apartment in, but the beam of the spotlight radiated around her like a glowing angelic beauty.

I didn't know if Billy saw it too. I imagined not.

She sat down at the piano, took one deep breath, and the club fell silent. Everyone waited for her to strike the first note before anyone could exhale.

When she did, the curtains from behind her opened to reveal a three-person band. The man nearest to us was the bassist. He paddled the strings with ease, swaying to the beat of the song. The drummer sat behind his Gretsch four-piece kit, tapping the snare liked a seasoned vet, and the man playing the Gibson hollow-body electric guitar plucked a rich solo before Cleo burst into song.

The moment she opened her mouth to sing the first lyric, I was thrown against my chair. Her resonant sound was so smooth—so powerful.

It was official, I was in love.

36

OVERHANGING TREES CROWNED THE DRIVEWAY IN A SHADOW as Mike shined his high beams deep into the property. When they came to a stop, the lights lit up the outside of the cabin.

"This it?" Kill said.

Mike nodded and shut off the engine. Kill stepped out and studied the surrounding area. Nestled amongst the trees, it was a perfect setting to stay off the radar.

"What do you think? Will this suffice?" Mike said.

The car lights illuminated the front door and Mike's face as he stood in the shadow of the car. Kill looked to him and nodded.

"Wait 'til you see the inside." Mike was exuberant—ready to show off the property.

Kill followed Mike up the stairs and onto the front porch. There were two rocking chairs resting there, pointed outward for a view of the entire property. Kill shifted his eyes away from the front door while Mike fumbled with the keys and the lock.

The headlights clicked off just as Mike unlocked the door. He reached inside and flipped on the light switch.

Kill stood by the door for a moment, until Mike said, "Get inside before the mosquitoes. Bastards are as big as birds in these woods."

Kill entered and searched the interior. The cabin was an open square. The living room, dining room, and kitchen were all jammed inside the space.

"Kitchen is well-stocked. Easily two month's worth of food up here." Mike led him to the pantry to show him. "I assume you know how to cook for yourself?"

"No. I have a cook make every one of my meals at home. He prepares everything for me," Kill said.

"Seriously?"

"No. Of course not, you idiot. I'm a grown man. I know how to cook."

"Easy, just saying. Some people don't know how. That's all."

Mike left Kill staring into the stocked pantry. It was full of mostly canned soups, vegetables, noodles, and other non-perishable items.

"Over there is a collection of books," Mike said from across the room. "Lots of spy novels and law thrillers. Some will be right up your alley in your current situation. May even find a plot similar to your own predicament in there."

That was Mike's way of being funny, but Kill didn't even crack a smile.

"Here's your TV. Not much to go on. Local stuff and whatever the antenna picks up. There is a news broadcast though, so maybe you can follow some local stuff in the area."

Kill walked toward the TV, but Mike didn't linger there. He proceeded down the hall and to the bedroom.

"Bedroom's here." Mike opened the door.

It was a small room, just big enough to fit a queen-size bed and two side tables.

"Bathroom's there." Mike pointed to the adjacent door.

Kill took in the space.

"Everything should be in order," Mike said.

"In order for what? For me to die of boredom?" Kill joked.

"It's either that or risk it on your own."

Kill huffed and walked back toward the kitchen area. In the living area there was a fireplace and above it, a shotgun.

"At least I can go hunting." Kill nodded toward the hanging gun.

"Just for show. No live ammunition."

"Well aren't you just full of fun facts."

"Sorry. But it's the best I can offer. Take it or leave it."

"You know I don't have a choice," Kill said.

"I know. I'm just messing with you."

"You're enjoying this, aren't you?"

"Damn right," Mike said.

Kill reeled and walked toward the kitchen bar as Mike walked toward the door.

Mike waited there, then said, "This is the last we'll see each other."

Kill had his attention.

"Keep this on at all times." Mike handed him a phone and charger. "I'll call you the moment your man is set free. When he is, I assume you'll receive another call from Mathis' source."

"That's the plan."

"Then I better get busy. I'm seeing the judge first thing tomorrow."

Kill swallowed hard, then nodded in agreement.

"I'll be in touch. Try to relax up here. It really is peaceful if you let it be."

"There's nothing peaceful about silence. It's more worrisome, than peaceful."

"Well then, I wish you luck." Mike chuckled, then said. "Look on the bright side, it's only for a few weeks."

37

In love? No. I couldn't believe what I was thinking. I wasn't in love. Not with Mathis' accomplice and ex-lover. It was just the music. It was so damn intoxicating.

I didn't even blink during the first song—not once. Only when people started clapping did I realize the song had come to an end. I shook myself out of the trance Cleo held me in and fell back hard on my chair.

"You okay over there?" Billy said. "Need a cigarette?" Apparently, he could see the adoration on my face.

"Stop."

"What? You didn't take your eyes off her. Sure, she's fine and all, but you were transfixed, my friend."

"No. I wasn't. It's just . . . the music—the atmosphere."

"Uh huh, yeah . . ." Billy didn't buy it. He took a pull from his beer and said, "Sure thing, Romeo."

A trumpet burst to life. A trumpet? I didn't see a trumpet on stage. But when I spun around, I saw the man that was playing the Gibson had set it aside and grabbed his brass horn. My eyes didn't linger on the trumpet long, because Cleo stepped out from behind her piano and took her place on a stool center stage.

Her soulful voice echoed inside the space, and she swayed with the song. Her look was so sultry, but still guarded by her shyness and she oozed feminine beauty.

Maybe it was the words of the song. She sang about loneliness and two lovers meeting in a chance encounter. The lyrics caused me to pause in my infatuation, because I couldn't help but think of Mathis. Was the song about him? About them?

My curiosity was piqued.

As the song continued, she talked about growing old together.

Not about Mathis.

Wait. I wondered if she knew about him. Did she know he was dead?

Two more songs passed before I slumped back into my chair. I hadn't even noticed Billy was gone. He was at the bar talking and laughing with a beautiful young twenty-something. He leaned on the bar, and she bent close to him. Part of me admired his easiness around women. The other part felt sorry for him, knowing he'd never find one to settle down with.

Then I stopped for a second and listened to my own inner monologue. Maybe I was the one in Cleo's song. The lonely man without a woman.

I needed air, so I stood and walked to the bar, leaned in behind Billy and said, "A word, please."

"Gimme a minute." He turned his attention back on the woman at his side.

"No. I need you now."

I crept forward, taking a few steps toward the door. I

knew he would follow. When we reached the entrance and walked outside, Billy barely waited until we were in the night air to say, "What the hell was that? I was in."

My back was turned to him. "I know."

"Then what the hell are we doing out here?"

"We need to talk to Cleo," I said.

"What—now?"

"Yeah. During her break."

"Why?"

"Because, I don't think she knows about Mathis. She can't. Not the way she's singing."

"What the hell does that mean?"

"She still loves him."

"And how do you know that?"

"No one sings with that much passion and desperation without holding love in their heart."

"What are you, some kind of love expert? What do you know about it? You're divorced."

I dropped my head.

"I'm sorry." Billy raised his hand and placed it on my shoulder. "I didn't mean anything by it, I swear."

"It's fine." I held up my hand and deflected, even though the shot was like a kick to the gut. "You're right, I am divorced. But I don't feel right about this. We need to tell her. Tell her that Mathis is dead."

"And you think that's when she'll give us the location of this alleged hidden stash of diamonds?" Of course, Billy had a point.

"I don't know. But I *do* know, if we withhold anything from her, she certainly won't give us the location."

Billy held his hands on his head and sighed—something he did when he didn't agree with my plans.

"You got any better ideas?" I said.

He looked to the ground and shook his head no.

"Good. Then we do it at her first break." I breezed by him just in case she was finishing up with her first set.

Before I entered, Billy said, "What do I do about the girl at the bar?"

I turned and grinned. "Drop her. I said no women."

I DIDN'T KNOW how long she sang for—not until I looked at my watch. She carried on for over an hour, and the time seemed to fly by in a blur.

"Thank you," she said shyly as the clapping subsided. "We'll be taking a break for about twenty minutes. So, grab your honey, hold them close, and warm yourself with a lowball of whiskey."

When she rose from the stool, I did the same. I grabbed Billy, who was still at the bar and talking to the same woman I told him to drop.

We watched Cleo walk off stage, followed by the band. They proceeded down a hallway and toward the back of the club. They turned the corner before reaching the back door. There was a bouncer guarding the back door to the club and the entrance to wherever Cleo and the band had just gone.

"You see that guy?" Billy yelled over my shoulder, but I only heard it as a whisper over the loud voices and the song on the jukebox. "He's huge."

And he was. Built much like Cleo's friends from the house in the bayou. In fact, it *was* the guy from the house, but where was his hulking bride?

He clenched his jaw when we got close. He recognized us as well.

"What'd you want, pig?"

"Pig? Really?" Billy said. "Isn't that a term of disregard for the police?"

He didn't respond as he stood stern.

"We need to see, Cleo," I said.

"Again? What about this time? The same bastard who took my boat?"

"No. He's dead," Billy said.

I eyed him angrily. *That's need to know.*

"Oh, really? Then what you want with her? If he's really dead, what you need to bother her for?"

"That's need to know," Billy said.

Oh, that's need to know? I shook my head at him.

"Look," I pleaded with him. "We just wanted to . . . to tell her in person about him. You know, let her down gently."

"She 'bout to go back on stage."

"I know." I grabbed his shoulder to empathize, but he took offense.

"Get your hand off me."

I retracted my hand like I'd been zapped by a bolt of electricity.

"Are you gonna let us back there, or what?" Billy was getting irritated.

"You got a warrant?"

"No, but I can get one." Billy stood tall and bowed up his chest.

The bouncer squared with him and waited for Billy to make a move.

"That's not necessary." I stepped in between Billy and him. "Like I said, we just want to talk to her. Tell her about

Mathis firsthand before she hears it on the news or reads about it online."

The bouncer lowered his guard and said, "I doubt she be interested in that news."

"Why's that?"

"Because she hated him."

"Obviously not," Billy said. "She got you to help him evade the police, the FBI, and the Marshal Service. I suppose that's something."

The bouncer was quiet now. I knew this was the time to make our move before he thought more and stopped us.

I crept away from him and looked down the hallway. There was only one closed door. That had to be where she was taking a break. And her break was about to be interrupted with news of a dead Mathis. How would she take it? According to the bouncer, she didn't care. But I knew that wasn't true. Not with the way she was singing.

38

I TAPPED ON THE DOOR. A MAN'S VOICE—A DEEP BARITONE—answered. "Yeah, what is it?"

"Uh, we need to speak with Cleo," I said.

The man opened the door, but only a crack. Both Billy and I could see inside. Cleo was sitting against the wall and the remainder of her band—aside from the one holding the door—sat next to her. They were smiling—maybe just coming out of a joke. But as soon as Cleo laid eyes on us, shock didn't linger on her lovely face—she expected to see us again.

"Can we speak with you?" I nodded to her.

Every man in the band waited for her to speak. They were close, that was easy to see. I assumed if she said to throw us out, the man holding the door would've had no problem with that task.

"What's this about, Agent James?" she said.

"Archibald Mathis." I expected the name to make her uncomfortable. For good or bad.

But she wasn't fazed at all. "Sure, come in."

Billy and I stepped through the door, and the three members of the band filed out, but not before giving us the stink eye.

When the door closed, Cleo stood from her seat and walked over to a fridge that sat in the corner.

"Beer?" she offered.

My mouth hung open. She was calm. Or maybe she was nervous and that was her way of calming her nerves. I held up my hand to say no, but Billy accepted her offer.

"Sure."

She grabbed a bottle and tossed it to him. I waited for her to sit before starting the conversation.

"You're really good . . . I mean . . . a beautiful singer," I said. What was I thinking? Why did I say that? I meant it, but still . . . it didn't need to be said.

"Thanks," she said.

I stalled, fumbling for coherent words. Even in the low yellow light, she transcended beauty.

"Tell me about Archie," she said. "Did you find him?"

I nodded yes.

"And?"

"I'm afraid, he's . . . he was shot. Killed in Clearwater, Florida."

She took in the news. But she didn't shed a tear. "By you?"

I shook my head no.

"Then you?" She turned her attention to Billy.

"No, ma'am. Some rat."

I shot Billy a look. He didn't have to say that. She didn't need to know that Kill was dirty.

She squinted and said, "What do you mean, some rat?"

I eyed Billy and shook my head no. But for some reason,

he didn't listen. He told her, told her everything that happened. About the murder. About our theory with the backpack. Everything.

"That's why you came here then, isn't it?" she said. "You think I have the backpack?"

"No. No, it's just . . ." I don't know why I said no. That was exactly the reason we came. Still though, I treaded carefully.

"You're damn right it is," Billy interjected. "Where is it?"

"Easy, Billy, come on." I motioned for him to lower his tone and hush up. Our approach wasn't working. No way she was going to give us the backpack.

But then two words escaped her pretty mouth—two words I thought I'd never hear. I mean, I had an inclination —a gut feeling, but . . .

"It's close."

"Wait, what?" I stared at her.

"It's close. Here. In this room."

Billy and I searched the area. Neither of us saw anything resembling a backpack. Then I recaptured Cleo's eye.

"What do you mean it's in this room? Where?" I said.

Cleo stood from her chair, walked to a closed door, opened it, and lifted the pack.

Billy and I stared in shock. No way, I couldn't believe my eyes.

Cleo floated across the room and toward us. She handed me the bag without a second thought.

My heart was in my throat in anticipation as I stared inside. The bag was full of rocks—uncut diamonds. Billy and I stared at each other for a moment, then looked back to Cleo.

"Why are you giving this to us?" Billy said.

"Because I need you to do something for me."

Name it. But I kept that thought to myself.

"What's that?" Billy said.

"A favor."

"What kind of favor?" I said.

"It's more . . ." She took a seat and leaned forward in her chair. "Call it, insurance."

"O . . . kay. What kind of insurance?" Billy said.

"Things have been set into motion."

I had no idea what she was talking about.

"What sort of things?"

"My brother will be released from prison shortly. I'd say . . . give or take about three to four weeks."

"Your brother? What do you mean released?" I said.

"A promise was made to Archie."

"What type of promise?" Billy said.

"As soon as my brother was released from prison, I would call the mole with the location of the diamonds."

"How do you know that?" I said.

"Because I received a text from Archie before he died."

"A text?" I said.

"Yes. A lengthy text, with very specific directions on how to proceed."

"So, you knew he was dead?" Billy said. "And that Deputy Kill was in on it?"

"Of course I knew."

I eyed Billy, wondering what was next.

"There's more," she said and rose from her chair, reaching out her phone and handing it to me.

"What's this?" I said.

"Read it."

I stared at the phone. The text was long, and it was from Mathis. When I looked back to Cleo she nodded, and I read.

Cleo,

I'm sorry. I know, I haven't . . . well, you know. I shouldn't have left you the way I did. That's my fault, and I'll never forgive myself for it. But maybe this . . . well, what I'm about to tell you will soften the blow a little.

Maybe.

Truth is, I bought a house for us in NOLA. It's registered under a different name so the feds can't track it, but I bought it for us. A long time ago. But I could never bring myself to come back to you. I was too ashamed of what I'd done. And now, here I am dying on the kitchen floor of a random stranger's house in Clearwater. I'd rather be back with you, in your arms, on your couch in the green room, our new house together or better yet, Belize. But that's not possible, not with the decisions I've made.

A man named Deputy Jack Kill is about to shoot me in the head. Apropos considering his damn name is Kill. That's unimportant, but what is important is the bag full of diamonds that's hiding in your dressing room closet. Don't bother looking now, it's there. I put it there after you left during our night of love making.

I PAUSED a moment and looked up at her. She wasn't blushing at all. Just standing there, watching me read—waiting for me to get to the good part.

INSIDE YOU'LL FIND *about twenty million in uncut diamonds. Take some. Whatever you want, there's more than enough for you to start over. Start a life somewhere away from New Orleans. If you want, that is.*

However, once Deputy Kill takes care of me, he's gonna want the location of those diamonds. So, here's what we're gonna do. He's going to get your brother out of prison. I know that's a shock, but when that happens, you need to call Kill to set up a meet. But it won't be you meeting him, it will be Special Agent Jasper James of the FBI.

MY BODY WENT RIGID. How could he know? Mathis planned the whole thing. He knew I'd come for her. I held my breath for a moment. Then continued.

HE'LL COME FOR YOU. I know him. And when he does, hand him your phone. Let him read everything I've just told you.

AGENT JAMES, I'm sorry for shooting you in the chest. But I'm glad you were wearing a vest. Truth was, that's why I didn't aim for your head. HAHA.

NOT FUNNY.

OKAY, not funny, I know. You were always the best man for the job. There were so many times you were close to catching me. But of course, I had Kill in my pocket and he helped me evade you every time. Now it's time for a gift. I set this up, the entire thing for you to capture the man who was really pulling the strings. This is your chance to put him in the ground, arrest him, or whatever you want to do with him. Just make sure he holds up his end by letting Cleo's brother out of prison. Make sure you protect her. Make sure she's safe. Because that's ultimately what I always wanted—her safe. That's all for me. Again, thank you, Special Agent James.

PS: Tell Cleo, I love her.

I STOPPED READING and stood dumbfounded. Billy saw my face and said, "What is it?"

My mouth gaped. When Billy ripped the phone from my grasp, I had to sit down while he read the text. It didn't take him long to read. Perhaps, Mathis' words shocked me more than him. Was Mathis truly sorry? How could he be? But that text changed things. Changed the way I thought about him all along.

"Is this true?" Billy looked to Cleo after finishing.

"Every word."

Billy sat down next to me and said, "Holy shit." He gasped. "Where does this leave us?"

Before I could answer, Cleo did instead. "With the man who murdered Archibald Mathis in the ground."

39

TWENTY-TWO DAYS LATER

The jail cells inside the prison were small—only one man to a room. In the mid-morning, Barrett Monroe was laying on his bunk after chow when a guard showed up outside his cell door.

Monroe saw him through the bars and could feel him hovering. He didn't say anything at first. Instead he kept enjoying a copy of Alexander Dumas' *The Three Musketeers.*

"I didn't know you could read, Monroe," the guard said.

"Better than you I suppose."

Monroe shifted in the bunk to put his feet on the floor, then stepped forward and waited for the guard to explain his sudden appearance.

"Mighty strong words. If you weren't getting processed today, I'd come in there and kick your ass."

"Processed?" Monroe was taken aback. "The hell you say?"

"I'm saying your release papers just came in. You're a free man."

Monroe gave the guard a confused look, then read the contents of the paper he held up. "Insufficient evidence?" Monroe questioned.

"That's right. Seems the sheriff planted something at the crime scene and pinned the crime on you. You're a free man."

Monroe was thrown for a loop. "Wahoo!" He clapped his hands.

"I guess, apologies are in order," the guard said, then nodded to someone out of sight. Another guard opened Monroe's cell and he walked out. "You just won't be getting any from me."

The guard grabbed Monroe and led him through general population lock-up, where other inmates were hooting and hollering. Some kind words were said, but mostly they threw insults. One man's voice rang through loud and clear.

"Monroe, I'll find you. And when I do, I'ma make you bleed."

Monroe saw the inmate and winked, then gave him a subtle grin. "Then I'll see you in about fifty years, huh."

The guard pulled Monroe through the corridor and the maze of doors that made up the prison. There were a set number of guard stations and a metal detector Monroe had to walk through before joining the free world again.

When they reached the processing station, Monroe was handed his personal items in a manilla envelope. The contents were minimal. One of the items was a picture of him and Cleo when they were kids at their grandparent's lake. He carried it with him always—always felt bad for leaving her behind. For what he did.

After gathering his belongings, he turned to leave. The

front doors were just ahead. He could see sunlight piercing through the glass. His insides turned—not in a bad way, but with excitement and anxiety of what his release from prison meant.

Before he reached the door, a man cut off his path. Warden Michael Dykstra was tough as nails, and he trained his guards to be the same. So it was no surprise to see him standing in Monroe's way one last time before he tasted freedom.

Monroe lifted his head high, waiting for one last taunt from Warden Dykstra.

"I'd say good luck, but I know luck has nothing to do with why you're in here."

"The hell you know?"

"I know inmates. They're like rats, they always come back for the cheese."

"The hell that mean?"

The warden laughed. "I figured you wouldn't understand that metaphor. But it's exactly the reason I'll see you again."

With that, Warden Dykstra stepped aside and allowed Monroe to exit.

Wind blew inside the door just as Monroe opened it, and the sun beat down and warmed his face. Monroe lingered for a moment. Even the air smelled sweeter as a free man. Like the lilacs were blooming in the spring just for him.

As he dropped his head and opened his eyes, he realized a man was standing close. He was dressed in a black suit. Monroe didn't know how any man could stand in the heat and not sweat through the material, but he did.

The man in the suit stood still while holding a briefcase in front of his body, then said, "Mr. Monroe?"

"Yeah, who the hell are you?"

The man in the suit came forward and said, "I'm the one that got you out of that hell hole."

"Uh, huh . . ." Monroe paused. "How's that?"

The man in the suit grinned but kept the information to himself.

"Let's just say we have a mutual interest in your release from prison."

"What's that mean?"

"It means I need you to do something for me." He reached into his pocket and lifted a cell phone.

"Hell no, man, I don't know you. I owe you nothing."

He chuckled to himself. "You have a funny way of saying thank you for getting out of prison four years, three months, and twelve days early."

Thrown, Monroe didn't know how to respond.

The man in the suit held out his cell phone and waited for him to take it.

"What you want me to do with that?"

"I want you to call your sister."

"My sister?"

"That's right. Cleo. Call her. The number is already programmed inside. All you need to do is press send."

Monroe eyed him funny. He couldn't help but wonder if this was a trick. But he did as he was asked, and no more than three rings later Cleo picked up.

"Hello," she said.

"Cleo. It's Barrett. Your brother," he said.

"I think I know who my brother is," Cleo said.

"Of course. Oh, uh, just wanted to tell you that I . . . just got released from prison." Monroe smiled.

"What? How? When?" She sounded surprised.

"Just now. I mean, right now."

"I'll come get you."

"No. No need." He switched ears, then stepped away from the man in the suit. "I'll . . . I'll get cleaned up first."

"Are you sure?" she said.

"Yes. I'll come see you soon. It's good to hear your voice, Cleo. I need to go now, so, goodbye."

"Bye. I'm so glad you're out."

"Me too." Monroe hung up and handed the phone back. "What now?"

The man in the suit lifted his sunglasses, then said. "I don't care what you do." He turned and walked back to his car.

"Wait," Monroe said.

The man in the suit turned and looked to him.

"What am I supposed to do?" Monroe said.

"Like I said, I don't care." He took more steps toward his car.

"Why did you get me out of prison then?" Monroe yelled.

The man in the suit stopped and spun around. "You were a means to an end."

"What's that mean?"

"I needed you to call your sister. That's all."

"My sister?" Monroe muttered to himself. He needed more answers.

Why would someone bother getting him out of jail to make one phone call to his sister? None of it made sense. But before Monroe could ask another question, the man in the suit disappeared into his black Lincoln and drove away.

40

I stood over Cleo's shoulder and helped her through the entire conversation. Of course, she needed to act surprised by her brother's release from prison. For effect, she couldn't give anything away—not to her brother, or the man who got him released from prison.

After she hung up, she looked at me for instruction. "Do you have Kill's number ready to go?" I said.

"Yes, I do. And Archie give me the address to our home."

"Go ahead and text him the location then."

I found Billy's eye. He was standing alongside Cohen, Duda, and our special guest, Sheriff Broxton. I wasn't gonna forget him, especially not then, not after the man who insulted him had turned out to be the one pulling the strings the entire time. He didn't have jurisdiction in New Orleans, but hey . . . I'm a man of my word.

I watched her type the address into the phone. She even showed me what she wrote before hitting send.

416 Eagle Vail Cir. New Orleans.

I nodded in agreement.

"How long do you think we'll need to wait?" she said.

Before I could even respond, her phone buzzed.

She read, then showed me the screen.

On my way.

"He's moving, people. Saddle up," I said.

"How long?" Billy said.

I eyed Cleo. But how would she know? Before I could ask her, she typed back and immediately received a response.

"One hour," she looked up and said.

"One hour," I repeated to Billy and those around.

As the team dispersed, I stayed with Cleo. She was still striking. Even if she had bags under her eyes from lack of sleep.

"You did great," I said.

"Thanks." She dropped her head.

I wanted to capture her gaze, get inside her head for a minute. "What's wrong?"

"Nothing." Again, she wouldn't raise her head.

"No, tell me," I pressed.

She paused. Maybe I shouldn't have pressed. I didn't know her that well.

"It's just . . . I want to see him suffer for what he did to Archie, but . . ." She trailed off.

"But what?"

"I feel . . . I don't know . . . kind of responsible for his death."

"Who, Mathis?"

She nodded shyly.

"Hey, come here." I wrapped her in a hug. Not my usual response to a woman in her position, but I knew she needed it. "You didn't. There's nothing you could've done. Mathis knew exactly what he was doing."

"Yeah, what's that?" she said.

"Protecting you." I just repeated the line from his text.

When we broke apart, she smiled. There was a twinkle in her eye, and a bolt of electricity ran through me as we locked eyes again. I stared at her lips, wanting to come close, but I knew that was foolish—in that situation or any other involving a woman like her. Still though, there was mutual attraction, I could sense it.

A car horn beeped and jolted me out of the trance.

"I better get going," I said, leaving her behind.

As I walked away, I couldn't help but grin. "Special Agent, James," she said, and I stopped in my tracks.

"It's Jasper." I spun around.

"Jasper." She stepped toward me. Then leaned on her toes and kissed me on the cheek. "Thank you."

Honestly, it caught me off guard.

Then Billy yelled out the window. "Come on, Loverboy, we got a US Marshal to arrest."

He was right. I blushed and headed for the car.

Inside, Billy stared at me—he wouldn't let the kiss die.

"What?" I said.

"You know what."

"No, I don't. What?"

"She kissed you."

"Uh, yeah, I was there, so what?"

"So what?"

"Yeah?"

Billy stalled for a minute. "I was just wondering when the last time that actually happened was." He busted a gut.

"It was with your mom," I teased him.

"Wait." Billy paused. "I thought that was in high school." Their laughter continued. "You haven't kissed anyone since high school."

"Shutup, you dick."

Billy had me. Always had the way of poking fun at my expense.

41

When we arrived at *416 Eagle Vail Cir*, we parked across the street from the house—a brown brick Tudor style manor with a brown roof, white paint, and brown trim. It was the first time I laid on eyes on the property. That was Cleo's idea. It wasn't because she didn't trust us—okay maybe it was. Still though, I trusted her and wanted to respect her desire to keep what she shared with Mathis private. Why wouldn't I? She—and Mathis—basically gift-wrapped Deputy Kill for us. She didn't need to either. Honestly, I admired her courage.

"Nice house," Billy said.

"Agreed."

I glanced at my watch. It had been almost forty minutes since Cleo texted Kill. With every passing second, my stomach turned. It was more than unsettled. I couldn't wait to see him walk into the house expecting to find a backpack only to find us: the FBI waiting to collect him with open arms when he tried to make an escape.

"Maybe we should move the car somewhere else. If Kill sees it, he'll know something's up," Billy said.

I nodded in agreement. "But how do we keep tabs on the house?"

"The alleyway." Billy pointed to the path that led away from Eagle Vail.

There were two cars parked there. Old and broken down. Easy to hide behind and they still had a sightline of the front door.

I nodded and got out.

"I'll dump the car and meet you behind that Ford."

After shutting the door, I moved toward the alley. As I kneeled, protected by the car, I still had a sightline of the front door. The longer I waited, the more my mind wandered. *Kill's gonna suspect something. Guaranteed. Hell, I would. He's not gonna just drive up on the curb like some amateur thief. He's got skills. Skills the government taught him.*

My muscles were tense, and I found myself scanning the rooftops of the surrounding houses for any sign of him. Like he was up there—some sniper—waiting to pick us off. My heart pumped wildly in my chest until I heard a voice over the radio.

"James? Where are you? Over," Cohen said.

"In position. Out of sight. Billy went to stash the car. I still have eyes on the house. We're regrouping any minute. Over."

"It's been forty-two minutes since Cleo received the text," she said. "Stay on alert. Call me when you have a visual. Over."

"Roger that. Over and out."

Footsteps pounded into the pavement behind me. My

eyes grew big and I spun, wielding my Glock and ready to shoot.

But there was no need, it was just Billy.

"You about gave me a heart attack." I couldn't calm my breathing.

"Little on edge, Jasper?" He grinned.

"Damn right. You're not?"

"Nah. We got this bastard."

"Do we?"

His face fell into distorted confusion. "What do you mean? Of course we do."

"Yeah, but he's been trained by the US Marshal service."

"So."

"So?"

"Yeah. So." Billy said. "He's blinded by greed. Clearly, since he capped Mathis in Clearwater, he only has one thing on his mind."

"Mathis was dying and Kill needed to get that information out of him."

"True. But trust me. He might do a little checking around the area before he goes into the house, but it's not like he knows we hooked up with Cleo and planned this entire operation. Technically, he didn't even know who he was texting. At least according to Mathis' last text to you on Cleo's phone."

Right.

"Look." Billy suggested I see who was coming.

Deputy Kill sauntered down the sidewalk and toward the house. He walked on the opposite side of the street from us, checking the area but keeping his eye fixed on the prize.

"We have a visual on Kill. He's approaching the house. Over," I spoke into the radio.

Billy was right, he never strayed from his intended target. Once he reached the steps of the front porch he stalled and gave one last glance to the street. Nothing was out of the ordinary. He walked up the staircase and reached for the handle. The door clicked open, and he stepped inside, shutting it behind him.

"Stay." Billy grabbed my arm.

"He's probably looking out the windows as we speak."

I wasn't stupid.

"Where are you guys?" Cohen came back over the radio.

"Uh, still in position in the alleyway, why?"

"Do you still see Kill? Over."

"Negative. He's inside the house. Do you want us to move in? Over."

"Negative. Not yet, not until we get into position on the opposite side of the house. Duda and I will be approaching soon. We will converge on the house together once he exits. We'll be in position momentarily. Over," Cohen said.

I was about to respond with a 10-4, but I didn't get the words out. I couldn't. Because the biggest, loudest explosion ejected me backwards and right into Billy's lap.

I scrambled to get my footing, and after I did, I stepped away from the alleyway and looked toward the house. The house was overwhelmed in a furious blaze. Fire crackled from every opening: the front door, the windows on the first and second level. The blaze couldn't be stopped. It couldn't be contained.

I stood frozen at the sight before me. Even from my position, I could feel the heat's intensity.

Billy waited by my side and said, "What the hell just happened?"

I was at a loss. Instinct should've kicked in, and I

should've ran for the house to extract the suspect. But I knew better—no way someone would've survived that blast. And as I watched the house burn, only one thought probed my mind. The explosion was set for one purpose and for one man alone.

"Mathis," I said.

"What about Mathis?" Billy said.

"He set this up."

"What? The fire?"

I nodded yes.

"How?"

"I don't know, but . . ."

"But what?"

Just as Billy asked his question, Cohen and Duda came barreling around the corner in their van. They sped past the home and directly at Billy and me as we stood watching the aftermath.

Cohen forced the door open, then slammed it shut. "What the hell happened, James?" She looked back at the fire.

"I . . . I don't know."

That was somewhat of a lie.

"What do you mean you don't know? Was Kill inside when the blast went off?"

"He was. Walked in and then five seconds later . . . boom," Billy said.

"I knew that bastard would get what he deserved," Sherriff Broxton said as he joined Cohen and Duda. "You guys have the coolest cases. I'm so jealous."

Cohen gave him the eye. "Shut it, Broxton."

"Sorry." His head fell.

Cohen huffed. "How did you let this happen? Did you

not canvas the house? Make sure it was all clear?" Cohen said.

That was the million-dollar question I knew she'd ask. I didn't want to give her my answer, but since she forced me to, it needed to be a strong enough argument to keep my job.

"Ma'am, we were given strict warning from our informant."

"Your informant? That's funny, James. By informant, you mean Mathis' ex-lover?" Cohen held her hands on her hips.

I nodded, then explained myself further. "She said to stay away out of respect for her and their relationship. This was supposed to be their forever home."

"Isn't that romantic," Billy added.

Cohen glared at him, then me. "And you listened to that bullshit?"

"We had no reason not to trust her." I kept digging myself deeper. "She handed over the diamonds. They're in our possession. The only thing left to do was fool Kill."

"Guarantee that sonofabitch didn't see a bomb coming." Leave it to Billy to try to lighten the mood. "I would've loved to see his face when the bomb went off."

"Can it, Lyons," Cohen said.

"I don't want to overstep here, but shouldn't we call the fire department?" Duda said.

Before any could answer, sirens echoed in the distance.

"Looks like someone already has," Billy said.

Within one minute, two fire trucks and three squad cars had converged on the area. We stood back and allowed them to follow their protocol. They canvased the area and of course approached us about what happened. After explaining ourselves and giving our credentials, they allowed us to stay, but at a distance.

The explosion opened another can of worms. Whose crime scene was it? Local PD? State? Ours? At the time, I didn't know.

WHEN THE EMTs wheeled out what was left of Deputy Kill, Cohen eyed me, but said nothing. Anger and disappointment lingered on her face. Sure we got our man, but not the way anyone would have expected. Cohen was going to have a lot of explaining to do, and I didn't envy her position.

After she got in the van and disappeared, Billy and I remained behind.

He lifted a cigarette and pulled one from his pack, then said, "There's no way Cleo didn't know this wasn't going to happen."

"What do you mean?"

After blowing out his draw, he said, "There's a reason she didn't want us to search the property. She knew it was going to blow."

I stared at the fireman who entered and exited the property. "No way. Not her." I was in denial.

"Yes, her. Think about it, Jasper. She warned us and we listened. Don't get me wrong, I'm glad we did, or we would've ended up in body bags like our old friend over there." He pointed at the ambulance. "I'm just saying, she knew."

And if she did, that would mean she was an accessory. But how the hell were we supposed to prove that?

EPILOGUE

WE DIDN'T EVEN HAVE TIME TO CHANGE OUT OF OUR GEAR. We sat in the van, waiting for nothing and staring at Cleo's front door. I didn't know why I was nervous, but I was. Maybe I didn't want to ask her the question. Maybe I didn't want to hear the truth. She couldn't be tied to the explosion; she wasn't part of the scheme. Mathis clearly concocted it on his own. But how could he? How could he set a trap from beyond the grave? Unless . . .

"You ready to go in?" Billy said and leaned forward in his seat, ready to grab the handle and exit.

"No, wait."

"Why?" Billy said.

"What if Mathis set this up before he left New Orleans?"

"What do you mean?"

"I mean, he was here for what . . . at least a few days before he fled for the Gulf."

Billy stayed silent for a moment, maybe calculating the timing in his head. "Yeah, sure. What does that prove?"

"I'm just saying, he could've planted the bomb before

meeting with Cleo and fleeing in the skiff."

"That's a stretch, Jasper. I'm telling you, your obsession with this girl is clouding your judgment."

"No, Billy, think about it. Mathis had the training and access to the property. He could've easily made it happen."

Again, Billy sat silent, until he said, "So what, he just planned on dying in Clearwater, then sent a text to his former lover, who would pretend the diamonds were at a specific property and lead Kill there so he could blow the bastard up? Come on, man."

"That's exactly what I'm saying."

Billy chuckled, then pushed the door open and walked into the day. "That's ridiculous, Jasper."

"No, Billy—" I wanted to continue my thought, but he didn't wait for me.

I followed him across the street, caught him on the sidewalk, and spun him around. "All I'm saying is, go in with an open mind."

"I am. Are you?"

Billy left me and didn't wait for a response.

He didn't have to. His point was obvious. I didn't move from the sidewalk until I heard Billy rapping on Cleo's front door. I jogged over to meet him and waited for her to answer.

There was clicking and the sound of unlocking a deadbolt.

After she opened it, I couldn't help but notice her hair was tied into a high ponytail and her clothes were stained with paint.

She was an artist. Of course she was.

"Agent James. Agent Lyons." She nodded, and there was excitement behind her eyes. "Tell me you arrested him."

See, Billy? Told you she didn't know about it.

"Ma'am, may we come in?" Billy said.

She opened the door and allowed us to enter without even thinking. Another sign of someone who was innocent. "Please."

Billy entered first. I followed him in and smiled at Cleo. She nervously smiled back. We waited for her to lead. She walked into the living room area where a painting was mounted on its easel. It was a beautiful rendition of a beach. White sand. Powder blue and turquoise water and a lone sea gull gliding through the perfect sky.

"That's beautiful." I nodded to the painting.

She looked down and blushed, then said, "Thank you."

We all stood awkwardly until she said, "Please sit. Can I get you anything to drink?"

We both sat on the couch, and Billy said, "No, ma'am. We just need to ask you a few questions."

"Uh, oh, that doesn't sound good." She grinned and took a seat of her own. "What kind of questions?"

Billy looked to me. I let him start the conversation, because honestly, I wanted to see where he took it.

"Deputy Marshal Kill was not arrested," Billy said.

She looked confused. "Um . . ."

"He was incinerated by an explosion."

My brow went up. Direct. But did I expect anything less from him?

Her hand went to her gaping mouth and she didn't speak. It seemed like the wind was sucked from her lungs. Again, not the reaction of a guilty party. At least none I'd encountered.

"Did you have anything to do with it?" Billy said.

"Billy." I grabbed his arm.

"What?" He looked over at me. "I just want to hear it from her."

"You can't think that I . . ." Her hand went to her chest. "I had something to do with that?"

"Why not? You said it yourself, you felt responsible for Mathis' death. And you wanted Kill dead."

"I . . . I . . ." She scrambled to defend herself.

"That's enough, Billy," I said.

Billy jumped from his position on the couch and paced the room. I waited and studied her reaction as she processed. The shock didn't leave her face. She was either an Oscar-worthy actress, a sociopath, or an innocent woman.

As he paced, Billy whipped around and found her again. "Let me see your phone."

I didn't understand why he was so demanding. My gut said she was innocent.

"What do you mean? Why?" she said.

"You warned us to stay away from the property. You knew a trap was set. You knew the bomb would go off. I need to see if Mathis texted you anything else about the house."

"Billy, we need a warrant for that," I said.

He shot me a death stare. She didn't know that was standard procedure.

"No, here, it's fine." She handed him the phone without a second thought.

Billy grabbed it from her hand and scrolled to her text messages. I watched him, then he handed me the phone. There was nothing written about the booby-trapped house. Only the one written to me and her.

"He could've told you in person then," Billy said.

"He didn't. I swear. I had no idea. I'm just finding out now."

"And how does it make you feel?" Billy said.

She was thrown. "What do you mean?"

"That Kill is dead?"

She remained silent and on the verge of tears.

It was time to move on.

"All right Billy, that's enough." I rose and grabbed his arm to lead him outside. "I'm sorry, ma'am."

I led Billy to the front door and left him there, then returned to the living room.

As I stood over her in the chair, I held out my business card. She looked up to me. "If you can think of anything, please don't hesitate to call me," I said.

Through teary eyes, she smiled.

"The local police might come by for questioning. If they do, you can tell them we already spoke to you about this."

She nodded.

I turned to leave, but before I did, she said, "Agent James?"

I spun around and looked to her. She rose from her chair, walked over to me, and leaned forward to kiss me on the cheek. When she pulled away, she said, "Thank you for avenging my Archie."

I smiled, then followed Billy out the front door. On the sidewalk, we gave one last glance at the house, and Billy said, "I still think she's involved."

"I know you do."

He walked away, but I lingered and stared at the door. Because if Billy was right, and we found out that she was involved somehow, I wanted to remember her for the innocent beautiful woman I thought she was.

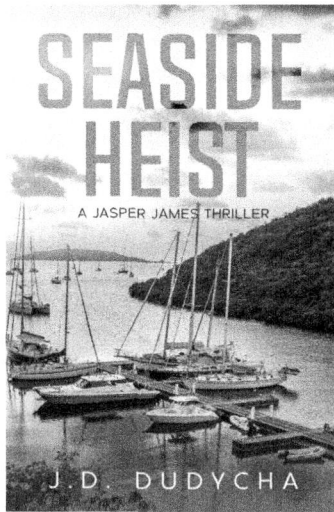

SEASIDE HEIST

By

J.D. Dudycha

PRE-ORDER TODAY!

Book two in the First Coast Adventure Series

Thank You Reader

Thank you for reading. If you enjoyed this book, I would appreciate you leaving a review on Amazon. Every review helps and I take great pride in what my readers have to say.

ACKNOWLEDGMENTS

To God be the glory. Without him allowing me to use my gifts, none of this would be possible. To my wonderfully understanding wife, Connie—you have allowed me to chase my dreams all the while keeping things together with our family.

To my remarkable editor, Josiah Davis—without you, none of this manuscript would make any sense. You have made this novel what it is today. To my beta readers—with your help, my story has begun to shine. And finally, thank you to my fans.

ABOUT THE AUTHOR

J.D. Dudycha believes the best stories are written with characters overcoming real life struggles and everyone deserves a shot a redemption. To get his debut novel for FREE, please visit his website: www.jddudycha.com

After a long stay in the baseball world, both as a player and a coach, J.D. has turned to his real passion, creating gritty, in-your-face characters who leap off the page and ooze practicality. You can't help but continue to read because you don't know where the story will take you next.

J.D. spends his time with his wife and children in the beautiful Rocky Mountains of Colorado. When he is able to step away from the world of writing fiction, he enjoys golf and fly fishing, and he never met a mountain he didn't want to climb or an ocean he didn't want to explore.

His inspiration is drawn from many different authors. Some of his favorites are C.S. Lewis, Clive Cussler, Lee Child, and Vince Flynn.

For more information visit:
www.jddudycha.com
Twitter: @JDDudycha
Facebook Page: www.facebook.com/jddudycha

Printed in Great Britain
by Amazon